CONFESSIONS OF A DANGEROUS FAE

JENNA WOLFHART

This book was written in the UK using British English, and the main setting is Edinburgh. Some spelling and word usage may differ from US English.

~

Confessions of a Dangerous Fae

Book One in House of Wraiths

CASTLE WRAITH

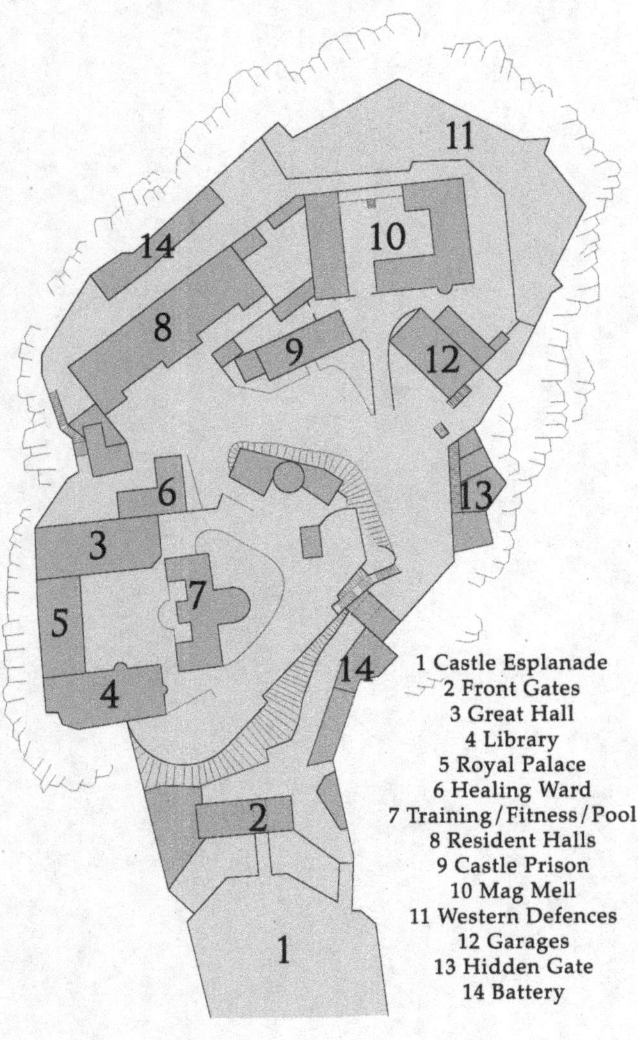

THE RAVEN COURT

Queen of Faerie
Clark Cavanaugh (The Morrigan)

The King Consort
Balor Beimnech (The Smiter)

Houses within the United Kingdom

House Beimnech (England)
Led by Queen Clark Cavanaugh

House Futrail (Northern Ireland)
Led by Master Tiarnan Breathnach

House Driscoll (Wales)
Led by Master Rhiannon Rees

~~House Athaira (Scotland)~~

~~Led by Master Athaira Archer~~
Court of Wraiths (Scotland)
Led by King Lugh Tuireann

Master is a unisex title that refers to fae leaders.
They defer to the Queen.

Solitary fae - a fae who is not a member of the
Court and is lacking the full strength of their
powers.

My sword tumbled into the sea.

"Bollocks," I muttered as I watched my beloved weapon vanish into the deep, swirling blue. My mission had just taken a massively wrong turn.

I stood on the swinging bridge that stretched between the Shivering Sands Fort and the Red Sands Fort, twin hulks of rusted metal that squatted on stilts above the Thames Estuary. It was the home of the Pack, and they didn't fancy hosting visitors for tea and biscuits.

To prove that point, they'd shifted into their wolf forms as soon as I'd stepped foot on the bridge. Of course, calling it a bridge was paying the thing a compliment I didn't think it deserved. With the rotting wooden planks and the thin ropes that served as handrails, it was more like a tightrope—one that might snap at any second.

"Who are you?" A shifter in the form of a man stepped out through the open doorway at the end of the bridge. Tall with wild, curly dark hair, grizzled, and built like a tank, Anderson had been the alpha of the Pack for the past two years.

He didn't recognize me, even though we'd met before. Thanks to my purple wig and pink contacts, I didn't look much like myself at all. I was Moira Talmhach, and my golden hair and matching eyes often gleamed in the night. It made me look very, very fae, as did my pointed ears I'd cleverly hidden beneath a bit of face putty.

Normally, I'd mask my identity by getting the assistance of a fae skilled in glamour. But we didn't have anyone with that ability at Court. Not anymore.

The loss of Elise, my best and oldest friend, my sister in spirit and soul, still left me with a hole in my heart. Even if we found a new fae skilled in glamour, I wouldn't ask him for help. It would feel like too much of a betrayal, even though I knew Elise would have given me a bemused smile and then told me I was being a muppet.

I sucked in a deep breath and shifted my attention back on the task at hand.

"Name's...Anna." Couldn't very well tell him my real name, now could I? The Pack here knew the names of most of us at Court. "I'm a shifter, too, and I heard about your place out here. I thought I'd come and check it out...?"

Anderson's nostrils flared as he took a long sniff. "You stink of feline. What are you, a cat?"

I reeked of feline because I'd spent the entire morning at a cat pub in London. I still had their fur stuck all over my jeans. Best way to convince a shifter you're one of them? Smell like an animal. Good thing I prefer cats to people. Of course, who wouldn't?

A low growl erupted from nearby, and I turned to spy a mangy-haired wolf that squatted precariously on the bridge. The pale moonlight glinted off his fangs. Shivers went through me, but I stood my ground. The Morrigan, my queen, had trusted me with this mission, and I would never let her down.

"Yeah, I'm a cat."

Anderson rubbed a beefy hand against his jaw. "You know you just stepped foot into a wolf pack, right? Wolves and cats don't mix."

While I'd been so focused on the wolves in front of me, I hadn't noticed the one behind me shifting back into his human form. He spoke up in a growl. "Why'd you bring a sword, eh?"

I shifted on my feet. My mind spun to come up with an explanation. "Okay, okay. I'll tell you the truth. Some friends and I were talking about this place, and they dared me to come out here and get inside. A thousand quid is on the line." I shrugged. "I'd do anything for a thousand quid."

Anderson's eyebrow winged upward. "And the sword?"

"I'm a cat sneaking into a den of wolves. I'd be a muppet to come unarmed."

"You're a muppet," the shifter from behind me snarled as he stepped closer, "to come at all."

I swallowed, hoping they couldn't hear the pounding of my heart.

"Actually." Anderson held up a hand. "I appreciate a dare. Takes moxie. Something most cats don't have."

I fought the urge to roll my eyes. Cats have plenty of moxie, evidenced by the deep gashes on my left arm. I'd petted a black kitten for too long, apparently, and she had been quick to communicate her displeasure.

"I'd only need to come inside for a minute." I tried on a smile, even though a scowl was my expression of choice most of the time. "And take a picture."

Anderson spun on his heels and waved for me to follow. Surprised, I minced across the rest of the swinging bridge, careful not to falter and tumble into the sea after my sword. The wolves skulked through the rusted door, clearly irritated that their night wouldn't end with a feline snack.

The alpha led me inside. The dimly lit hallway ended at a large room that had been fitted as a living area. I glanced around, impressed. They'd done a lot of renovations on the place. Gone were the rusted walls and stained yellow carpets. Instead, a gleaming hardwood floor reflected the wrought-iron sconces that hung along the plastered and painted walls.

I'd been here once before, hence the disguise and the whole feline shifter story. I didn't want the werewolves to know that I'm fae.

Relations between our two factions were…troubled, to put it mildly. That had a lot to do with the werewolves dipping their toes into criminal waters. Rumours had been flying for months. No one knew exactly what they were up to, but tales suggested it was nothing good.

And I was here to find out exactly what they were doing before it caused the entire supernatural community a heap of trouble. Humans had known about all of us for years now, but the world was still tense and on edge. We needed to play by the rules to keep the peace.

"Right. You're inside now. Take your picture." *And get out* were the unspoken words that followed.

Anderson waved a hand at the living area. The biggest television I'd ever seen hung on the far wall between two thin windows. Several leather sofas were clustered around it, along with a few armchairs and bean bags. An antique rug covered the floor. It was pretty cozy. But it wasn't what I had come here to see, and I needed to find a way to get a better look around.

"Wicked." I held up my phone and snapped a pic. "Mind if I use your toilet? I downed a pint before rowing out here. For moxie. I need a wee. Bad."

Anderson frowned but then gave a nod. He pointed at a hallway on the opposite end of the room. "Three doors down and on your right. But make it quick. We have some Pack business to attend to, and we can't have any cats lurking around."

My ears pricked up. Pack business. That sounded promising.

I shot Anderson a grateful smile—fake, of course—and hurried out of the room. Another dimly lit hallway stretched out before me. This one hadn't been renovated like the rest. Rust clung to the sagging walls. Lightbulbs flickered like something out of a horror film. The stench of dirt and salt swirled through the cramped space. I wrinkled my nose and ducked into the loo.

I kept the door cracked but flicked on the lights —and almost gagged. Mildew spread across the cracked linoleum and a yellowish gunk filled the sink. The toilet lid was shut. I had no intention of opening it. No telling what I'd find inside.

Instead, I pressed a hand against the doorframe and turned my ear toward the hallway. I slowed my breathing, focusing on the distant murmur of voices. My enhanced fae hearing sparked to life like a rush of adrenaline through my veins. Everything around me dimmed. The feel of the rough wood beneath my hands faded until it was a dull shape against my fingers.

"We don't welcome fae here." The voice was rough and familiar. Anderson. A chill went through me. I thought I'd convinced the alpha of my story. The last thing I wanted to do was run. The only way out of here was to vault out of the window and plummet into the churning water below the fort. I'd done it once before, and it hurt like hell.

Another voice spoke up in response. Smooth and melodic with a heavy Scottish accent. "I was told you're willing to sell to any bidder, regardless of their supernatural origin. If not, I'm happy to take my money elsewhere."

I let out a tiny exhale. So *that* was the fae. Not me. I could tell by the strange otherworldly tremor of his voice. Shifters don't sound like that. Neither do vampires. Humans especially don't.

Which begged the question…why was another fae here?

I turned my attention back to the conversation.

"No, no." Anderson cleared his throat. "Just tell me what you're after, and I'll see what I can do."

"A cauldron," the fae answered.

I furrowed my brow. Like, a sorcerer's cauldron? What would a fae want with one of those?

Anderson let out a low whistle, and I winced. High-pitched noises were excruciating when I had my enhanced hearing turned up to maximum. Like nails against chalkboard, only ten times worse.

"The name of this cauldron happen to be what I think it is?"

"Most likely."

"So, it's true then," the alpha replied, his voice gruff. "The Scotland fae are plotting against the Morrigan. You lot want to steal her crown."

A finger of ice slipped down my spine, and the corners of my vision went dark. The Morrigan was the Queen of the fae. *My* queen. If someone was plotting against her…

"I'd rather not share what I plan to use it for," the fae crisply replied. "Can you find it for me or not?"

"This may take some effort. And time." I heard the scribble of a pen on paper. "This is the quote for my services."

My breathing went shallow as my brain whirred with this new information. I understood Anderson's operation here now. He found things and delivered them to the highest bidder, and it wasn't technically illegal unless the objects themselves were inherently dangerous.

And it sounded like this cauldron was.

I needed to find out more.

Just as I pressed myself closer to the crack in the door, light splashed on the rusted hallway floor. I sucked in a breath and stepped back but not before a pair of black boots followed the light. Twin ominous shadows stretched out behind them. I dragged my eyes up. A fae unlike any I'd ever seen stood before me.

He was impossibly tall with midnight blue hair, horns curving out of his head, and eyes that were as dark as ravens. The angles of his face were sharp and strong. Slim but well-muscled, his black shirt clung to him like a second skin. Power radiated off his body and curled toward me, wisps of his magic lingering against my neck.

I found it hard to breathe.

He smirked. "Lost?"

I shook my head and slammed the loo door on his face. My heart raced so fast that I had to sag against the wall to catch my breath. What the hell was wrong with me? So what if I'd been caught spying on Anderson's visitor? No big deal. A nosy shifter kitten would have done the same bloody thing.

Their conversation echoed in my mind. Forget about photographic evidence. I needed to get back to the Court. That fae was plotting against the queen. And judging by the look of him, he wasn't going to be easy to beat.

2

I stood in the throne room before the queen, also known as the Morrigan. Or, in my case, just Clark. We'd been friends before she'd ascended to her throne two years ago, and I rarely followed the protocol of titles. She didn't mind, and it was one of the things I liked about her. She'd give her left arm—and then her right one for good measure—for any one of us, and then she'd buy us a pint.

"Moira, what's wrong?" She stood from her throne, a wooden chair with a carved pair of raven wings that flared out on either side. It signified her bond with the birds. Clark was half-shifter instead of full fae. Most of the fae didn't mind, though some clearly did—like this mysterious male I'd run into at the fort. Her reign had not come easy, and it wasn't exactly surprising there were still those out there who might rebel.

I'd tossed the wig in the bin on my way to the throne room, and my golden locks hung in loose waves around my shoulders. "I found out what Anderson is up to. You're probably going to want to call in the others."

She searched my eyes and then turned to the male beside her. Her husband, Balor Beimnech. The two of them were mated, giving them a bond that most fae spent their entire lives dreaming of.

Not me. I hoped I never met my mate.

Muscular and brimming with power, Balor was one of the strongest living fae alive. Clark gave him a slight nod, and he strode out of the room without another word.

A moment later, he returned. With him, he'd brought the "managers" of the royal guard stationed in London. Kyle, a skinny, wiry male who was our resident computer expert. Ondine and Eoin, who took care of general security matters and paperwork, and Ronan, who wasn't even a fae. He was full shifter—a wolf—but he'd sworn his allegiance to Clark.

There were many more members of the royal guard than this, but they were on duty, patrolling the grounds, watching the security cameras. Some were on missions, like the one I'd just done, to keep on top of supernatural activities.

Clark gave a solemn nod to each of the guard team. "Moira has some news she'd like all of us to hear."

I took a deep breath and filled them in on everything I'd heard. It didn't take long for the team to start peppering me with questions.

Who was he?

Is he part of House Athaira?

What else did he say?

I threw up my hands. "I don't know. He was literally on his way out the door, and I couldn't exactly ask Anderson these questions. He was suspicious enough when they spotted me eavesdropping."

"What about the name of the cauldron?" Clark asked. "If we could find that out, Kyle could do some research for us."

I shook my head. "They never said it out loud."

"Right." Clark nodded. "It's settled then. We need someone to go to Scotland and find out what this fae is planning. Find out what this cauldron is and make sure he doesn't get it. And Moira, I would like that someone to be you."

~

*B*ack in my room, I packed my bag. I didn't need much. Just a few changes of clothes and my toiletries. Even if I ended up staying longer than a few days, a spy mission wasn't the kind of trip where hauling around a heavy suitcase was very practical.

I glanced around when I was done, heart constricting. This place was my home. At the

Court's home base in London, several hundred fae resided in the old Battersea Power Station that had been renovated into a beautiful residential complex. It was kind of like university halls, only fancier. Floor-to-ceiling windows overlooked the sparkling lights of London, and a four poster bed hunkered beside antique artwork I'd collected over the years.

I'd lived here for a very long time. Everything I knew, everyone I cared about, was here.

I didn't want to leave, even if it was for only a little while.

A light knock sounded on my open door, and Clark poked her head through. Thick, wavy strands of brilliant red fell into her eyes.

"Mind if I have a moment?" she asked quietly.

I waved her inside. "'Course not. I'm glad you came by."

She strode through the door and handed me a thin, long object wrapped in a black cloth. As soon as I felt the weight of it in my hands, magic zoomed through my veins, giving me a sudden burst of adrenaline.

"A sword." I arched a brow. "An old one, if the feel of it is any indication."

"To replace the one that fell into the sea." She gave me a meaningful look. "Can't very well have you going on a spy mission without your gift to back you up."

Every fae is born with one power, magical or otherwise. Mine is skill with the blade. No one had ever bested me in a one-on-one sword fight. Not even the queen herself.

I smiled and propped the sword against the wall. "Thanks. Mind if I ask you something?"

"You can always ask me anything. You know that. I might be the queen, but I am first and foremost your friend."

I swallowed hard and stared at the floor. That was why this entire thing was so difficult. "Why are you sending *me*? Why not one of the other guards? I'm good at swinging steel. Not spying."

Amusement flickered in her eyes. "How can you say you're not good at spying when you've just sneaked into Pack headquarters and found out that a mysterious fae from Scotland is making plans to use some kind of cauldron against me?"

I opened my mouth, but then snapped it shut. "Okay, you have a point, but…"

Clark stepped forward and put her hand on my shoulder, squeezing tight. "But what, Moira?"

"You keep sending me out on missions, away from the Court," I said insistently. "I swore an oath to protect you. The best place I can do that is here. By your side."

Clark's smile dimmed. "I thought filling up your time would give you some purpose. You haven't been yourself since Elise died."

Elise. My heart constricted, and I closed my eyes. The pain still felt as fresh as it had the day Nemain, a sociopathic fae hellbent on the throne, had murdered her. That day, it had felt like half of my soul had been ripped away from me. It had never come back.

"I think it would be good for you to get out of London," Clark continued. "Besides, I don't trust anyone with this mission more than I trust you. You're the best of us, Moira."

I winced and tried to give her a smile. Little did she know, I was anything but.

~

I took the train to Edinburgh. The Court was wealthy enough to afford the flight, but the rail had far less of a paper trail. I'd left my wig in the bin and had gone for natural makeup. The traitor—which was what I was calling him in my head now—had only seen me for a fleeting second, but I didn't want to take any chances he would remember a purple-haired fae lurking in the loo.

When I stepped off the train and onto the platform at the station, a heavy mist immediately descended all around me. A chill sank deep into my bones. I buried my hands in the pockets of my leather jacket and turned my feet toward the castle.

The formidable castle that loomed over Edinburgh was home to House Athaira, the first stop on my tour of hunting down traitors. If he lived in this area, then he was most likely one of the many fae who called the castle home. Back when there had been seven courts instead of one, House Athaira had been part of the court in London. They had always been loyal to the crown. Until recently. They *had* sat idly by while Nemain had attacked us all.

Maybe it was because they'd been plotting against us all this time.

As I approached the castle, it was all I could do not to stop and stare. It was an impressive sight. Squatting on top of ancient volcanic rock, the stone fortress was protected by sheer cliffs and tall battlements that stretched all around. A slight tremor went through me. I had next to no idea what I would be walking into, and the place looked far more ominous in person than it did in the photographs I'd studied on the train.

With a deep breath, I continued the climb up the stairs and across the ancient cobblestones. Finally, I reached the castle. The arching double doors of the gatehouse were shut tight. On either side, flickering torches lit up the night. Over the door, three tiny windows looked down on where I stood. The middle window was covered by an elaborate shield, decorated with a sigil. One I'd never seen before. It was a cloaked figure surrounded by a full moon.

I strode forward and eyed the gargoyle knocker. Its teeth were bared and claws outstretched. Frowning, I tried to push open the door, but it wouldn't budge. So I tried a knock instead. A moment later, the heavy wooden monstrosity creaked open to reveal a petite brunette fae with purple eyes. Eyes that I swore looked deep into my soul.

She gave me a glance from head to toe before resting her gaze on the sword sticking out of my bag, still hidden in the folds of the black cloth. "What are you doing here? You aren't a House Athaira fae."

What a greeting.

"Nope. I'm a solitary fae. I'm sick of being on the run, and I want to check out your House."

The fae's nose scrunched up. Solitary fae weren't exactly popular. Outcasts and outsiders, they spent their lives alone. It was a terrible way for them to live, partially because the magic kept them from having access to the full strength of their power. Just like the shifters, we did better as a pack. Being solitary meant you existed. Being part of the Court meant you thrived.

"I'm sorry. I can't let you inside," she said in a strong Irish accent. She took a step back and made a move to close the door.

"Wait." I stuck out my boot to stop her from shutting me out completely. "At least let me talk to your Master."

She sniffed. "You mean King Lugh."

I tried to hide my surprise. There were no *Kings* anymore. No Princes or Princesses. Only Masters. They kept things chugging along at their individual Houses and reported directly to the queen, who had brought all the fae together under one rule. And this fae did not want me to come inside. Alarm bells clanged in my head. Something strange was going on in Scotland all right. And that something started right here.

"Erm," I said slowly. "I thought the leaders of the Houses were called Masters."

"House Athaira is different. Wait right here." She shut the door in my face. Well then.

I frowned at the brass gargoyle knocker. Maybe I'd be better off finding a window I could climb into, although this castle was infamous for being impenetrable. These fae were clearly hiding something here, and they didn't seem responsive to strangers.

I took a step back to look for some other way to sneak inside, but the door swung open before I could get far. It was all I could do not to gargle out a swear. The fae who stood before me now had midnight blue hair and a jawline that could cut through steel.

King Lugh was the fae I'd seen in the loo.

3

"*H*ello," he said smoothly as his dark eyes drank me in. Just as the female had, he rested his gaze on my hidden sword. "Saoirse tells me you're a solitary fae in need of a home. I'm Lugh, Master of this house."

"King," Saoirse hissed beneath her breath.

"Master will do for now."

My mind whirred. Okay, so the guy who'd met with Anderson and had asked for the cauldron was none other than the Master of this House. And he was either calling himself a king, or his subjects were insisting upon it. Maybe both. He was after some kind of magical cauldron, and he planned to use it to steal the crown from Clark.

At least it hadn't taken me long to find the right guy. Now I just needed to stop him.

To make matters even stranger, I *knew* the Master who lived here. Or I thought I did. Her name was...well, it was Athaira—she'd named her House after herself. This lad, Lugh, I'd never heard of.

"Something the matter?" he asked in that lilting Scottish accent of his.

"You're not what I expected," I admitted. "Some friends told me about this place, and they didn't mention a king."

"No, I don't suppose they did." His dark eyes flashed as he turned toward Saoirse. "Leave us. I'll take it from here. Oh, and call a meeting in the Great Hall."

A strange unease prickled the back of my neck. "What's the meeting for?"

"You'll find out soon enough, if I agree to it." Crossing his arms over his chest, he leaned against the stone doorframe. "Before I let you inside, I need to ask you a few questions."

"Okay." I mimicked his stance. "Ask away."

"What's your name?"

"Moira." I figured I'd go with the truth. He'd never met me, and I'd never met him.

"Pretty name." His eyes slightly narrowed. "Why are you here?"

"I told you why I'm here. Why are *you* being so mysterious?" I shot back, unable to help myself. "I thought the Court was eager to help solitary fae. Strength in numbers, you know."

"Oh, *I* know." He straightened and took a step forward. His shoulders loomed over me, and I swore magic sparked between our bodies. "But how do *you* know? I was under the impression that solitary fae knew little about Court customs."

"I did my research."

"Hmm." He tapped his chin. "Are you willing to sign an NDA agreement?"

"An…NDA agreement?" My mouth dropped open. This was absurd. In all my time as a fae, which was a hundred years now, I'd never heard of such a thing. We were *fae*, for fuck's sake. Bound by duty and honour. We didn't need things like NDA agreements.

"That's right. A contract, signed in blood."

"I…" My heart skipped a beat. A blood contract. Those were rare and took a very special type of skill in order to pull them off. I hadn't known that House Athaira even had a fae with that kind of power. Seemed they were keeping far more secrets than one.

A malicious grin spread across his face. "Your choice. Either you're in, in which case you sign the contract, or you're out."

I stared at Lugh. He looked like a villain in a film, all sharp lines and immovable steel. He had presented me with an impossible choice. I could enter this castle and find out what he had planned. But then I wouldn't be able to tell a soul. Blood contracts are forever binding. If I found the truth inside these castle walls, how would I get the information to Clark?

My queen's words—my *friend's* words—rang in my ears. *You're the best of us, Moira.*

I wasn't. Not even close. But maybe I could prove I was better than the worst.

The only way to discover Lugh's plans was to infiltrate his castle. To do that, I would have to sign a blood contract. But the great thing about magic is, there's always a way out. A counter spell, a loophole, something. I'd figure something out.

With a deep breath, I gave a nod. "I'm in."

~

Turned out it wasn't as simple as signing my freedom away on a blood contract. Lugh paraded me through the cobblestone courtyard and then into a Great Hall packed to the brim with tittering fae. The large, expansive room rose to a hammerbeam roof made with dark timber, rounded off in decorative stone-carved corbels. Flickering sconces highlighted the collection of swords that were hanging in rows by the entry. The bottom half of the walls were glistening wood, polished to perfection. The top half had been painted crimson red.

Twenty rows of wooden tables spread from one end of the room to the next, facing the front where a throne made of twisting black vines sat on an elevated stone dais. Behind it, flames roared in a dominating fireplace.

My stomach flipped as I stared. He'd fashioned himself a throne. This was worse than I'd thought.

Lugh strode through the packed hall with his head held high, his hand curled tightly around my arm. He practically dragged me forward. Whispers and murmurs rose to a harsh crescendo. When we reached the front, he deposited me at the front of the dais. He settled into his throne and crossed his ankle over his leg, leaning back with a smug smile.

The room fell silent with a hush.

My heart thumped as I scanned the crowd. They all stared at their king in awe, eyes shining with eager anticipation.

"Welcome to the House of Wraiths. We are ghosts, spectres. The rest of Faerie does not know we exist." Lugh flicked his fingers at a small squat hobgoblin who scurried out of the shadows.

I swallowed the lump in my throat. It had been decades since I'd seen one of these creatures. I thought most had died during the plague, and the rest during the human world wars. They were strange little fae. This one was male, with greenish skin, a long snout, and ears that were as big as his face, pointing up toward the ceiling. He was about as tall as my waist, but his feet were three times the size of mine.

The hobgoblin that scurried toward me wore a billowing black cloak and nothing else. Even though I knew he was harmless, I had to fight the urge to step back. They could be vicious when they wanted to be.

I slid my eyes from the hobgoblin to King Lugh. *House of Wraiths?* Not only was Lugh calling himself a king, he'd changed the name of his House. I had enough information to go straight to Clark now. I could just sprint out the door and never look back. Of course, I still didn't know what Lugh had planned. And I didn't know what the cauldron could do.

The hobgoblin shoved an ancient parchment into my hands with words written out in an elaborate scrawl. His little voice was high-pitched when he spoke. "This is your blood contract. It binds you to never speak of this place or what you find within it."

He held out a pen, waiting.

Bracing myself, I grabbed the parchment and signed my name.

The hobgoblin let out a screech, and the entire hall joined in with the cheer. I glanced from one wicked grin to the next, wondering what the hell I'd gotten myself into. These were not welcoming faces. They weren't applauding because they were happy I'd joined their House of Wraiths. I knew that sparkle in their eye. I'd walked straight into some kind of trap, and the hammer was about to fall.

The hobgoblin sauntered over to King Lugh and shoved the contract into his hands. A moment later, Lugh whisked it out of sight. The little creature strode from one end of the raised dais to the next, hands tucked neatly behind his back. His over-sized ears swished from side to side. Suddenly, he stopped and whirled toward the crowd with a dramatic flair that only hobgoblins possessed.

"Every new member of the House of Wraiths must undergo a trial to prove their worth," the hobgoblin said, his wicked eyes flashing. He glanced at me over his shoulder. "What is your gift?"

I let a beat pass, and then another. I didn't want to tell this room of fae my power, but I didn't see a way out of it, either. "I'm skilled with the blade."

Out of the corner of my eye, Lugh shifted on his throne. The hobgoblin looked delighted. A murmur even went through the crowd. Great. Just what I needed. They were excited about this— about the way I could handle a blade. That never led to anything good.

"We could use a warrior," the king murmured.

"Very well then." The hobgoblin clapped his hands and turned toward the crowd once again. "It is now time for you, my dear House of Wraiths, to vote on the trial that Moira must endure to join us. As always, you will be given three options. The first of which is this: Moira must slay as many vampire mannequins as possible within five minutes. She must beat the current record, set by our king himself."

Mannequins? Sure, okay. No problem at all. That seemed fairly straightforward and not nearly as gruesome as I'd expected. I shot a glance at the king and tried to take a measure of his skill. He was clearly strong and formidable. I wouldn't want him to sneak up behind me in a shadowy alley. His muscular physique confirmed he spent hours training for time in the field. But what was his skill? If it wasn't swordplay, his record didn't stand a chance against me.

Much to my disappointment, only a few hands shot up at that option.

"Brilliant." The hobgoblin's smile stretched wide. "Second option, Moira must fight our strongest warrior. The winner is the first to draw blood. Injuries are encouraged."

I shifted on my feet and frowned. The first to draw blood? Injuries encouraged? While I had no doubt in my abilities, the trial was quickly trans-forming from a harmless display of strength to a blood-soaked battle.

Much to my relief, only a few hands shot up once again.

The hobgoblin twisted to face me and grinned. At the look in his yellow-green eyes, unease clenched my stomach. Suddenly, I understood what was about to happen. If the pattern followed, this next option had something nasty in store.

"It seems the third option wins by default," the hobgoblin began with a cackle. "And that option is…Moira must descend into the Sluagh vaults. All she must do is survive."

~

"*Y*ou didn't say anything about me fighting a bunch of bloody Sluagh."

Hands propped on my hips, I shouted the words at Lugh.

After the vote, he had smoothly led me out of the Great Hall and into some sort of staging room where he now examined my sword with a disturbing amount of apathy. The room was empty apart from the two of us and some folding chairs. The only door had been barred shut, and no windows provided a view out of this hellhole.

Lugh shrugged. "If you find this trial too daunting, you are free to leave."

My mouth opened and then closed. Damn him. Sluagh were nasty creatures. Dangerous and vicious and made from pure evil. They were basically the walking dead, but stronger. They knew how to wield weapons, and they'd do anything to tear out someone's eyeball. I could take on a few by myself, but an entire vault full of them? No, thanks.

He lifted his eyes from my sword. "What will it be? Decide carefully, Moira. If you walk away, you will not be allowed back inside this castle."

"You made me sign a blood contract."

"And?" He arched a brow. "The contract says nothing about allowing you to join this House. It does not bind us to you. It only binds *you* to us and limits your freedom to speak of this place."

I ground my teeth together. That would teach me for not reading the entire bloody thing.

"How many Sluagh are down there?" I demanded.

"I honestly don't know," he said. "The vaults are swarming with them. The path you must take will likely bring you into contact with a couple dozen. If you're lucky."

Furious, I stabbed a finger into his chest. "A couple dozen? You honestly expect to put a new recruit through something like this? It could get me killed."

Or worse.

"Careful." His voice was as smooth as chocolate as he pulled my finger away from the black shirt that clung to his chest, but his eyes flashed with danger. "I wouldn't want to have to call my guards."

"Right. Like you need their back up." I swallowed hard when he kept a tight grip on my hand. "Who the hell are you anyway? Where's the old Master of this House? What's up with the House of Wraiths? I've never heard of a fae named Lugh. I know I'm an outsider, but I'm shocked rumours haven't spread about what's going on here. You've made up your own bloody House, one not recognised by the rest of Faerie."

His smile stretched thin, and his hand tensed around mine. "My name isn't known because I do not want it to be. And the truth about our House is in the name. We are wraiths, Moira. The world outside these ancient stone walls does not know what we do in here. And if you pass this trial, you'll become a wraith, too."

A shudder went through me. His words both electrified and terrified me. I wanted to take him down, more than ever, but I also wanted to run screaming in the opposite direction. *Wraiths*. That name invoked terror and death. Visions of nightmarish forms in hooded cloaks flashed through my mind. Memories I thought I'd hidden so deep inside me I'd never have to remember them again.

Furiously, I blinked those images away.

"Let me guess." He dropped my hand. "You want to back out of this trial. It's too dangerous for you to handle."

"No." I bristled. "I've fought Sluagh before. Easy peasy."

His dark as night eyes widened, and he suddenly looked keenly interested. Too keenly. "When would a solitary fae have fought the walking dead?"

I wrapped my belt around my waist and grabbed my sword from where he'd leaned it against the wall. "You don't know what it's like out there. Not when you're sitting up here in your fancy castle, doling out dangerous trials to fae who simply need a roof over their heads."

For a fleeting moment, I thought about ending this entire thing right here and now. I had my sword. He had no weapon, at least that I could see. None of his guards were in here, and I had a pretty good idea the route I'd need to take to find the exit door.

It could be over before he took his next breath.

Silence hung between us, heavy and loud. The world slowed around me as my magic caressed the sword strapped to my side. The steel seemed to pulse in time with the beat of my heart. We were in sync. That was how it worked. It knew everything I thought, every move I wanted to make. It would be in my hands, and I wouldn't even have to blink.

"I'm going to call for my guards now," he murmured, his eyes never leaving my face, as if he could read every single thought going through my mind. "What's your decision? Are you going to run? Or are you going to stay and fight?"

A flush crept up my neck, and I didn't know why. Instead of calling to my sword, I just stood still. Why didn't I go ahead and take care of him now? One flash of steel, and it would all be over. One slice of my sword, and I could be down the hallway, heading for the exit door.

But even if I'd slain many enemies, I'd never killed a fae in cold blood. If I chopped off his head in this room, without hard proof of his crimes against the crown, I'd be just as bad as his traitorous arse.

I lifted my chin. "Call them. I'll fight."

His eyes flashed, and I could have sworn his shoulders sagged—just a bit. He almost seemed disappointed. Had he hoped I'd back down and scurry out of here with my tail between my legs? That only made me want to show him up even more. Not only would I survive these vaults, I'd do so in record time.

Unless the Sluagh ate me, of course...

As soon as he cracked the door and called for his guards, new unease roiled through me. Why, oh why, did it have to be the Sluagh?

Anything else. Vampires, werewolves, sorcerers with insane spell-casting abilities. Hell, even fae, like this one. The Sluagh were the one thing I feared more than anything else, except for those night-marish figures in my mind, figures I'd tried so hard to block out. The *real* wraiths.

"You're looking kind of pale." Amusement shone in Lugh's dark eyes. "Not cut out for the job?"

"Maybe if you doubt my skills, you should fight me yourself," I shot back.

A thrill went through me when he crossed the room. My chest constricted as I was forced to drop back my head to meet his eyes. Somehow, the distance between us had vanished. Only a single sheet of paper could fit between our bodies, and I could practically feel the beat of his heart syncing with mine—syncing with my steel. His magic curled up my neck, sliding across the delicate skin beneath my ear.

I refused to shudder, even though my body begged to shake. I wouldn't let him see that kind of response.

"That is awfully tempting," he said in a low growl that sent skitters of hot magic down my spine. For a moment, I held my breath, half hoping he'd volunteer to fight me and half dreading he'd make that call.

The door pushed open, and several fae spilled into the room. The power pulsing between us snapped away. Lugh, smirking, stepped back and turned toward his subjects. One was the purple-eyed door greeter, Saoirse. Two more were fae I'd noticed standing solemnly in the back corner of the Great Hall, a female and a male, both with fiery hair. They were clad in all black with swords strapped to their backs. Warriors, no doubt.

Lugh zeroed his attention in on Saoirse. "Well?"

She gave a quick shake of her head. Lugh frowned, and then tsked.

What the hell did that mean?

He turned to me, his eyes flashing. That blood-curdling magic shot through my veins once again. "Very well then. Moira, it's time for your trial."

4

The vaults were dark, dreary, and creepy as hell. I'd been given a tiny headlamp and one instruction. Make it through the maze of tunnels and reach the exit two hundred metres to the east. Easy peasy. No big deal.

I cast a glance over my shoulder at the cluster of fae watching me. Saoirse looked alarmed. The two ginger warriors looked smug. And Lugh? His expression screamed boredom. Not for the first time, I asked myself why I hadn't just stabbed him with my sword when I'd had the chance.

He saw me watching him, and his voice dripped with derision. "Last chance to back out. If you don't have the courage, speak up now."

I prickled at his words. This male was such a tosser. How he'd managed to worm his way into being the Master of a House was beyond me, let alone been given the title of King.

"Oh, I'm not bloody backing down now," I shot back. "Tell me though, Lugh, you ever fought dozens of Sluagh yourself?"

Saoirse shifted on her feet uncomfortably, and the warriors settled their hands on the hilts of their swords. But the bored expression on Lugh's face never wavered.

"Doubting your future king's abilities?"

"Well, I don't know much about you, do I?" I shrugged. "Maybe you're skilled in something like gardening, and you've never seen combat yourself."

His eyes flickered. "What a unique skill you've chosen to point out. I know there is a fae in the Morrigan's court who has a way with plant life. But there would be no way for you to know that, would there?"

Our gazes locked. Was he trying to imply something? Was he suspicious of my motives? If he was, why would he give me the chance to join his Court of Wraiths?

"Like I said. I did my research."

He stepped closer, ducking his head beneath the low stone doorway that led into the vaults. As he came closer, so did his magic. It wrapped around me like a too-tight hug, squeezing the air out of my lungs. "Yes, I can see that you are a fae who likes to be prepared. Is that why you're stalling now?"

"I'm not stalling," I hissed at him. "I just want to know who you are."

He dropped his face closer to mine and growled

into my ear. "I am Lugh, King of the Court of Wraiths. And if you wish to become my subject, you must learn when to stop questioning me."

He stepped back, sucking all his body heat along with him. A part of me ached to pull him back. Just so I could punch him in the eye.

"Enough." Lugh ducked out of the vaults and flicked his fingers at the two warriors. They moved forward, grabbing the heavy wooden door and slamming it in my face. Heart beating, I stood there for a moment staring at it. Even though I'd known it was coming, I still didn't feel prepared. They'd shut me in with the Sluagh.

My hands clenched, and I turned to face the long stretch of corridor before me. The headlamp flickered, threatening to plunge me into darkness. I tapped it. The beam of light stayed strong. Blowing out a hot breath, I began to inch my way forward.

Lugh had explained that there would be several forks in the vaults. I was always to take the right, no matter what. So, when I came to the first bend and two tunnels stretched out on either side, I went right.

My feet splashed into deep puddles of water. Grime ran down the crumbling stone walls. The stench of mildew and rot swirled through the corridors, and I had to swallow down the need to gag.

Why the hell had Lugh made me do this? Hell, the entire court had chosen it. They'd seemed eager to see me sweat, almost like they were a Court of

Wankers more than anything else. I had only been alive long enough to remember the mortal realm, this realm. But I'd heard stories of a time before this, when our kind held court in a different realm. The fae realm.

Back then, we'd been cruel. We'd been wicked. We'd been harsh.

The fae in this castle seemed to be remnants of that time. Especially Lugh. The bastard.

I came to another fork, and took the right again. My breath misted before me as I crept forward even more. This wasn't so bad. So far, I hadn't seen a single bloody Sluagh. Maybe they'd moved on from these vaults and found some other underground hellhole to stalk.

But just as my relief started to build, a strange scuttling noise whispered through the darkness. I paused, breath held. Flicking my ears toward the sound, I listened again. More scuttling, along with the hiss of papery breathing.

Terror speared my heart. That noise was unmistakable. The Sluagh were up ahead.

Maybe there was another way to tackle this Lugh problem. Maybe I could get the information we needed through a different kind of mission. I didn't need to risk my life to prove to Lugh that I was worthy of his acceptance. I could turn around right now and get the hell out of here.

But how would I take him down? He had clearly holed up in the castle. All of his secrets lay within.

He'd made me sign a blood contract, for fuck's sake. If he went to those kind of lengths to protect himself, I'd never be able to get close to him without being a member of his court.

I sucked a deep breath in through my nose and steeled my nerves. I was Moira Talmhach, and I was a bloody good warrior. These Sluagh wouldn't stand a chance against me.

I inched forward, step after slow step. The Sluagh didn't have hearing as good as mine, so they likely didn't know I was down here with them yet. I wanted to keep it that way for as long as possible. The element of surprise was one of the only tricks I had in my bag, especially when I had no idea how many of them there were.

Lugh had mentioned dozens, if I were lucky. These vaults were the perfect playground for the walking dead. They were dark, musty, and full of rats. No sunlight could get to them here, and Sluagh tended to disintegrate when rays of sun touched their skin.

On that note...I flicked off the headlamp, and the world turned pitch black. No need to advertise I was here. Steadying my breathing, I focused my fae power on my sight. The world became a bit brighter but only just.

A Sluagh rounded the corner. It hissed, and I stumbled back. Even in the darkness, my enhanced sight gave me a full view of the creature. The skeletal frame hobbled toward me on feet that were half-covered in rotting flesh. It stank of disease, like a pile of excrement dipped in a vat of stagnant water. It reached out toward me and screamed, mouth open wide to reveal of pit of darkness inside.

Swallowing hard, I held up my sword before me. My heart ricocheted through my chest. My palms were slick with sweat. It had been a long-ass time since I'd seen one of these things, but the terror it brought was all the same.

It lurched toward me, and I whirled to the right. My side slammed into the slick wall, and pain radiated from the bruised skin. Gritting my teeth, I pushed off the wall and charged.

Magic swirled through my veins as I tightened my grip on the sword. My body became one with the steel; the feel of it hummed beneath my hands. Grinning, I stared down the Sluagh. It had slowed to a stop as my magic coursed through my body like an electric charge.

Before the creature could turn and run, I rushed forward. My sword arced through the air, and then made contact.

The Sluagh's rotting head fell to my feet.

One down. How many more to go? There was no telling.

After wiping my sword against my jeans—I refused to fight with the Sluagh's blackish blood on my weapon—I came to another damn fork in the path. How many tunnels did these vaults have? It was a fucking maze down here.

Just as I turned toward the right once again, my ears flicked. They caught some distant sound, coming from the left. Frowning, I paused. Somewhere, down the left path, the clanging of steel echoed.

Instinctively, I took a step toward it.

What the hell was going on? Had Lugh sent another recruit down here to complete the same damn trial as me?

The guy was a sociopathic jackass, but that didn't make much sense.

Another Sluagh lurched out of the tunnel to my right. Just in time, I swung my sword up to block the weapon it held in its hand. The steel of the creature's blade sang as it met mine. My heart thumped as I took a step back. That was a fae weapon. A gleaming sword that rippled with the magic coursing through its hilt.

Before the Sluagh could swing again and hit me with whatever magic lay within, I stabbed it right in the gut. Black blood oozed onto my blade as the creature fell into a bony heap.

The distant clang of steel met my ears again. Frowning, I took a step down the left path. A muffled grunt echoed toward me, and a strange scent filled my nose. Fire and something like pine cones, drifting along the musty wind. I cocked my head. Someone else was down here, alright, but who?

A loud screech shot through the darkness. I

whirled on my feet to find five Sluagh now bearing down on me. They must have heard me fighting the others. And every single one of them had blades.

Gritting my teeth, I slashed at the first. It fell to the ground within seconds. I ducked low as the next rushed toward me, its vacant eyes staring right into my soul. They continued on. And I kept fighting. One after another, I sliced. Up ahead, in the distance, the tunnel on the right speared with light. I could see the doorway. I'd finally made it.

There were just ten bloody Sluagh in the way of safety.

I slowed to a stop, chest heaving. As I'd fought, I'd somehow made it into a domed room. Black blood caked the walls. Grime seeped into my boots. The exit door out of this hell sat on the opposite wall, light seeping through the cracks.

The Sluagh stared me down. Their mouths were opened wide, their clawed, bony fingers clutching tight to various blades. Some held daggers, carved in elaborate designs. Others held up swords, rippling with magic and danger.

I sucked in a deep breath and focused. More than ever, I needed my gift. Curling my hand tight around the golden hilt of my sword, I let my eyes drop shut, just for a moment. The steel sang to me, a brilliant sound that lit up every vein in my body. Adrenaline surged through me. Electricity shot through my core.

I opened my eyes. The Sluagh were coming for me. But I was ready.

I slashed through the first, and then the next. My body became a whirlwind, spinning so fast that I didn't even know the moves I made. I trusted in my gift, my magic. It would carry me through, even if nothing else could. I didn't think. I didn't even breathe.

All I did was fight.

Soon, all the Sluagh were dead. Chest heaving, I sucked in a deep lungful of blood-soaked air. I wiped the gunk off my blade and shoved it into the sheath around my waist. Up ahead, the exit door practically glowed like a beacon. I'd taken on this damn trial. And I'd won.

I tried not to look at the ground as I toed my way through the bloody pile of bodies. Some were merely crumpled heaps of bones. But some were far more than that. I didn't want to look into the eye of anyone who looked even remotely like the humans they'd once been.

When I reached the door, I let out a relieved sigh. This whole thing had sucked some serious ass, but it could have been a lot worse. I hadn't died, for one. And I hadn't lost a limb. A few scratches and bruises were nothing compared to what could have been.

I reached for the door and screamed. A fleshy hand had wrapped itself around my ankle, squeezing so tight I swore my bone would pop. It yanked with a terrifying strength, pulling me to the ground. I fell hard and my teeth slammed together.

It took a second for me to get my bearings.

A second too long. The Sluagh scrabbled on top of me and pinned me down on the stone. I writhed, twisting and turning and trying to knock the thing off. It stank of rot, and I gagged.

As I threw my weight upward at the Sluagh, it barely budged. This creature was strong. Too strong. The only way I was going to get out of this was with my sword. Gritting my teeth, I twisted my arm toward my sheath, but the scrabbling Sluagh made it impossible for me to do anything but claw at the dirt.

I stared up at its hollow eyes. There couldn't be much intelligence in there. Time to try a different option.

I reached up and grabbed the back of its head. Sucking in a deep breath, I slammed my forehead against the Sluagh's. Pain licked through my face, but I'd achieved my mission. The Sluagh stilled, swaying back and forth like a lifeless doll.

I grabbed the Sluagh and flipped over, straddling its gruesome form. Now there was nothing standing between me and my sword. I reached for it, but another bony hand closed around my skin. Another Sluagh had appeared. It wrenched me away from the one I'd trapped and threw me toward the wall with a frightening force.

I hit the wall hard. My head smacked against

the stone. I fell into a heap, legs twisting beneath me. Several more Sluagh stormed into the vaults. And they were heading right for me.

The one who had thrown me jumped on top of my reeling body and pinned me to the ground. Another joined it. And then another. Soon, I was stuck, and bony hands wrapped around my throat.

I thrashed and thrashed but it was no use. I couldn't move. I definitely couldn't breathe. I choked against their fingers, gasping for air. Darkness crept into the corners of my vision, threatening to pull me under. Tears stung my eyes.

I was going to die here. Down in the filth. All alone. The way I'd always feared I would go. Pinned down, trapped, with no one but me.

My consciousness slipped away until all I could see was the rage-filled face of the Sluagh who was killing me. And then the silver-tipped spear that sliced through its skull.

~

Coughing, I rolled over and cracked open my eyes. My throat was on fire. It felt like a million tiny daggers had raked down my oesophagus. I lifted my hand to my skin and felt the indention of fingers. Memories suddenly flooded my mind. The Sluagh choking me. The spear that had slammed into its head.

I was on my unsteady feet within seconds. My

hands found my sword. I raised it before me. The half dozen Sluagh who had pinned me to the ground now lay dead all around my feet.

My heart thumped hard as I glanced around me. What the hell had happened? Where had that spear disappeared to? And where the hell had it come from?

Gingerly, I stepped over the bodies, still glancing from one mottled face to the next. Not a single one of these Sluagh had a spear sticking through its skull. Someone had been down here. They had killed the Sluagh. And then they'd fled.

But *who*?

I didn't have time to dwell on it because another scuttling sound shot out of the darkness.

"Don't bloody tell me there's another one of these things," I muttered out loud.

And sure enough, there came another Sluagh, creeping along like a wraith in the night. I held up my sword and narrowed my eyes.

"Yeah, I don't think so, mate. I am so done with this damn trial. You come near me, and your head will be on that floor with the rest of the dead."

Unfortunately for the creature, it took no heed of my warning. It still wanted to eat me. So, as soon as it stepped foot within the swing of my sword, I whirled. Steel met flesh, and it fell. The head thumped with a sickening crunch.

In the distance, the rush of scuttling Sluagh feet answered.

"Yeah, no. Fuck this." I shook my head. "That is *it*."

Maybe my Spear Friend was still out there, watching and waiting, but I wasn't going to stick around to find out. Plus, I could save myself, thank you very much. All I had to do was open that damn door.

With my sword still clutched in my hands, I booked it across the room. I grabbed the handle and ripped open the door. Four pairs of eyes peered down from above. The door opened into a brick wall, with a platform all the way up to my eye level.

I cast a glance over my shoulder as the rush of scuttling feet grew louder.

"I see you're alive...just barely." Lugh's voice was as apathetic as ever. "Why have you opened the door? It sounds like there are several more Sluagh down there who are eager to fight you."

Narrowing my eyes, I sheathed my sword and reached for the platform edge. "You said my task was to get through this hellhole of a maze without dying. Well, I've made it. I refuse to stay down here for even a second longer."

Surprisingly, he didn't argue. He took my hand in his and pulled me out of the vaults. I hated how strong and steady he felt, and I especially hated how relieved I was to see him.

"You look like shite," he said with a grin as he pulled me out of the vaults just in time. He slammed the door shut behind me, trapping the Sluagh inside.

I glared at him.

His voice was smooth, like syrup. "Welcome to the Court of Wraiths."

5

Covered in stale water, grime, and blackish blood, I gratefully followed Saoirse through the residential hallways of Castle Wraith—which I'd learned it was called. Turned out these fae were huge fans of the whole wraith thing. Her long brunette hair swished at her waist, her stride confident, her demeanour unbothered. She really didn't give a toss that I'd almost died an hour ago.

King Lugh had barely given me a word of acknowledgement after he'd hauled me out of the vaults. He'd merely welcomed me into his Court and then vanished like the wraith he was. A part of me had wanted to chase him down to see what he was up to...but I had to admit, I needed some rest. My entire body ached from the fight.

Saoirse stopped at a doorway identical to the others about halfway down the hallway. After pushing it open, she motioned me inside. The room was much larger than the one back home, and the furnishings far less posh.

All the walls were wood, including the lofted ceiling. A single bed had been placed in the corner beside a tiny window. A pair of thick red curtains hung loosely, skimming along a threadbare rug that matched. A vase of red flowers perched on a small, square bedside table, along with a hotel-like phone and a ticking clock. In the opposite corner, an antique desk sat before a wooden chair. A couple of floor lamps glowed from each end of the room, casting shadows onto the television hanging above a small cupboard.

Other than that, there wasn't much to see. It was sparse and mismatched, but cosy in a way I hadn't expected.

"This will be your new home." She spread her arms wide. "You're lucky. This room only opened up a few weeks ago. If it hadn't, you would have been given one of the cold ones on the top floor. The heating isn't working up there right now."

I cocked my head. "Why did it become available?"

She pressed her lips together. "Ah. That's a long story. Maybe it can wait until tomorrow."

Interesting. More secrets. More unanswered questions. I filed this one away with the multitude of others I'd collected since I'd stepped foot through that yawning front gate.

I took a stroll around the room and stopped at

the tiny square of a window. It was only big enough for one of my feet to punch through it. I peered outside at the foggy, blurring lights of the city streets down below the steep cliff. If I ended up needing a hasty exit, this wouldn't be it.

"You have any questions?"

"I've gotta ask." I picked up a remote control I spotted on the bedside table and spun it in my hand. "Did everyone here have to go through that?"

She nodded emphatically. "When we decided to become the Court of Wraiths, we all did a trial to prove we belonged here. That said, most of the original trials were easier. It all depends on your gift. And outsiders have it the worst. Sorry about that."

"Lugh was the one who decided to form the Court of Wraiths?"

"Not really." She shrugged. "It was a group decision. We want to do our own thing and not answer to the Morrigan. You must feel the same way, or you wouldn't have gone through the trial, right?"

I swallowed. I hated speaking against Clark, even if it was a lie. "Why else would I be here?"

She gave a satisfied nod. "Then, you'll fit in here just fine. Though...I should warn you. Some of the fae here can be kind of...difficult with outsiders. It's only because they don't know you. They'll come around in time."

Great. So, this was the Court of Mean Girls. Just what I needed.

"Hmm." I dropped the remote on the bed and glanced around. "Why all the secrecy? I mean, I get that you made a court that you wanted to hide from the rest of the fae, but you seem to have gone to a lot of trouble just for that."

I hoped I wasn't pushing it, but I didn't see how I'd ever get the answers to my questions unless I asked. Sure, hiding an entire damn court with its own damn king was a pretty big deal. But there seemed to be more going on here. Lugh was hiding something *massive*. I was certain of it.

Saoirse's purple eyes flickered, and she took a step back toward the door. "You're part of the Court of Wraiths now, Moira. That's going to have to be enough for awhile."

I frowned. "What does that even mean?"

"We don't know you yet," she pointed out.

"Yeah, but I just went through a dangerous trial." I gestured at the tiny window I could never escape. "I'm in this thing, one hundred percent. I even signed a blood contract."

"And that will have to be enough," she insisted. "You'll find out more when Lugh decides you're ready. I can tell that you think he's a cruel king, but you don't know what he's been through...nevermind."

I opened my mouth to ask what she meant, but she shook her head.

She pushed open the door, and then paused. "You'll find a shower room in the door to your left.

In the cupboard beneath the telly, there are shelves stocked with snacks and a mini-refrigerator with drinks. If you need anything, dial zero on your phone."

Before I could say another word, she quietly shut the door behind her. A lock tumbled into place. My heart racing, I crossed the room and tried the handle.

The Court of Wraiths had locked me inside.

~

A knock sounded on my door. Groaning, I rolled onto my side to glare at the clock. It was six in the morning. My entire body ached from the previous night's fight. My skin felt raw from where I'd been bashed against the stone walls, my throat was on fire, and I had a headache straight out of the underworld. Fae heal fast, but we're not invincible. It would take a few more hours for all my bruises to fully mend, and another day for me to feel like my normal self.

Before I could stumble out of bed, the pesky knocker opened the door.

Lugh strode inside, looking frustratingly perfect. His hair was freshly-washed, damp curls dropping onto his forehead. I could tell he'd shaved, but he'd left enough stubble to highlight his sharp jaw. His dark eyes raked over me, alert and unbothered.

If I'd been more awake, I probably would have gaped.

"You're still in bed," he said with an air of displeasure.

I sat up and brushed my matted hair out of my face. I'd taken a long, hot shower before crawling into my bed last night, damp hair tied back in a loose bun. The strands were dry now, but they had escaped from the elastic in the night. I didn't have to look in the mirror to know I had the worst case of bed head imaginable.

I blinked up at him through fuzzy eyes. "Sod off. I'm knackered. It's not even daylight yet, and I spent my night trying not to die. If a girl deserves a lie in, it's now."

"You won't be punished because I realise you're accustomed to life as a solitary fae, where you can do whatever you damn well please." He sniffed. "But here, in the Court of Wraiths, we don't waste our precious time with sleep."

I arched a brow. Or I at least tried to. It was probably more like a half-assed wiggle. "Oh yeah? Then, what do you waste your precious time with?"

Because as far as I could tell, the Court of Wraiths merely specialised in making my life a living hell. And that didn't require getting up at the crack of dawn. All they had to do was toss me into the vaults with the Sluagh...and someone else.

That got me thinking a little more clearly. What the hell had even happened last night? There'd been some other mysterious fighter in the vaults. Someone with a spear. I wanted to ask Lugh about it. Surely he'd know if someone else was inside of his castle, fighting those creatures.

But I couldn't. If, for some reason, it had nothing to do with him, I couldn't let him find out. If he knew I had help staying alive, he might decide I'd failed my trial. And then I'd have to leave. Empty-handed.

Lugh cleared his throat as he slid further into the room. "We each have a daily assignment. It keeps the castle running as smoothly as possible."

Ah, so Lugh had at least kept *some* of the courtly customs. Back in London, it was the same. Some assignments were far less involved than others, but every single fae had a purpose. Mine was obviously guarding the queen and working alongside others to keep the Court safe from harm.

If I could do the same here, I could easily get the inside scoop on Lugh's plots and schemes.

"You know my skill. I'm a warrior. I'd probably do best in some sort of guard role," I said smoothly.

"I'm afraid that won't be possible." His dark gaze swept across me, and a strange tremor went through me. "While I can't deny your skills must be exceptional in order for you to make it through the vaults, you are still very new to our Court. You'll find that it takes quite some time for the fae here to trust outsiders."

I blew out a frustrated breath. "Isn't that what I

signed a blood contract for? So that you could make sure I couldn't spill your secrets? Surely that's good enough to put me on watch duty in a tower or something."

"You're pushy." He strode closer, his eyes flashing. His magic seeped from his body, lighting up sparks along my skin. "I don't like it."

I suddenly became very aware that I was in bed wearing nothing more than a white t-shirt and no bra underneath. At some point, Lugh had shut the door behind him, and we were trapped inside this room alone. It made my heart pound, though I didn't know why. Sure, he was as fit as sin, but he was scum.

As he strode closer and a wicked smile played across his lips, a strange thought flittered through me. A thought I wished I'd never had. It made me want to burn my brain.

I was an outsider. A stranger. Lugh didn't want to trust me, even if I'd signed that contract. Something about me must have made him uneasy. Best way to quieten his doubts?

I wet my lips.

I'd been approaching this whole thing in typical Moira fashion. Pissed off and eager to stab something. What if instead of communicating exactly how much I hated him, I made him think I wanted him? Right here beside me in this bed.

"If you don't like it," I tried, adding a sultry tone to my voice, "why do your eyes say otherwise?"

Blimey, that sounded like nonsense. Like something out of a cheesy porn film. Not that I'd ever watched one. Ahem.

He dropped to his knees beside my bed and curled his palm around my cheek. I shuddered, magic ripping through my gut so fast I could barely think. "You have a very purple bruise on your face. It's disgusting."

My mouth fell open. That gormless swine.

"Did you come here just to insult me?" I hurled. "Or was there some other reason you decided to drag me out of bed at six in the morning?"

His lips quirked with amusement. "What a brilliant idea."

"What?" I shouted just as he threw the covers off my bare legs. He wrapped his hands around my ankles and pulled me out of the bed in one fluid motion. I fell flat on my bum, glaring up at him, my t-shirt hiked up around my hips.

I jumped to my feet, my body trembling with anger.

"Careful," he said with a smile. "If you lay a hand on me, I might have to call my guards. Of which you aren't one." His smile widened at the furious part of my lips. "You will be joining the cleaning staff. I hope you're as good with a broom as you are with your sword."

~

ortunately, Lugh left before I ended up punching him right in his beautifully-chiselled face. And, as it turned out, I didn't have to start my new cleaning duties just yet. As soon as Lugh disappeared into the hallway, Saoirse bustled inside to explain the day ahead.

"We have a party every time someone passes a trial," she said excitedly. "I wanted to tell you last night, but I thought you'd be too pumped to sleep."

Too pumped to sleep because of a...party? Damn. I eyed her enthusiasm warily. These fae really didn't get out much.

"You'll be able to meet everyone, and you can get a tour of the grounds." She passed me a large black box. "Until then, you're going to have to stay in here."

"So I still can't leave my room. What a surprise," I said dryly.

"Don't worry," she quickly interjected. "It won't be for much longer. We just don't have anyone to chaperone you for most of the day since we'll all be getting ready for the party."

"Chaperone?" I shook my head and tossed the box onto the bed. "Don't you think that's going a little far?"

"Rules are rules." She shrugged. "Newbies get chaperoned. See you tonight."

The rest of the day passed in a mindless blur. I paced from one end of the room to the next, the restlessness in my body building with every second that passed. I tried the door handle at least two dozen times, but the lock didn't magically open for a single one of them. I peered out the tiny window, sighed, and then peered some more.

It was one of the most boring days of my life. A surprise, since I was a secret spy in a court of wraiths. You'd think I'd have a tad more action than this.

Shortly after nightfall, Saoirse collected me from my room. While I'd been bored out of my mind, I'd found a gown in the black box. A sleek black number that did little to hide my toned curves. My makeup, I'd kept natural, and my hair no longer hung loose around my shoulders. I'd pulled it back into a high ponytail instead.

I topped off the whole look with my signature black boots.

Saoirse, clad in a flowing green dress and pointy high heels, slowed and let out a low whistle. "That outfit is a *choice*."

"I learned a long time ago that a girl should always be ready for a fight. And I can't swing a sword in heels."

She laughed. "This is your party. You won't be expected to fight."

"That's a shame." I grinned.

Saoirse didn't seem to know what to make of that, so she breezed me out of the room. "On our way, I'll point out some of the highlights of the castle. For example, down at the end of that hallway, you'll find a flight of stairs that leads up to the roof. We aren't allowed to go up there."

"Of course you aren't," I said with a roll of my eyes. But, that was potentially important information, and I made sure to make a mental note of it.

Saoirse led me out of the residential quarters and into a tiny, squat building. There were fewer windows in this section of the castle, and gloominess swirled through the narrow hallways, along with clouds of dust. With a smile, Saoirse bustled forward and pointed out the highlights. In this building, three fae healers had set up a room for the injured. Further on, I'd find the storage room for blankets, pillows, toilet rolls, and towels.

After the short tour, we continued on to a courtyard I'd seen last night. Here, there were four adjoining buildings that made up a square. Saoirse took me into the one that sat on the right of the Great Hall and pointed out an expansive, gleaming kitchen. It had stainless steel work surfaces, more like a restaurant than a home.

She slowed to a stop to point out a smaller room to the left of the kitchen where round tables dotted a carpeted floor. "This is the kitchen and a smaller dining room. Most evening meals we have all together in the Great Hall, but you can come here and grab breakfast and lunch on your own."

"Except I can't," I said dryly. "Not without a chaperone."

"In time," she whispered fiercely, and then continued on. She pointed to the right as we passed another door. "Big laundry room in there. You can do it yourself, or you can ask one of the cleaning staff to do it for you."

Right. So I could ask *myself* to do it then.

At the very end of the hallway, we came to a stop outside of two double doors, but Saoirse didn't make a move to open them. "This is the training room. Our warriors spend a lot of time in here."

I gave a nod and yearned to push inside. I already missed the training room back home. My muscles ached with the need to move. To swing my sword. To practice my breathing. To hold my body as still as a tree while I focused my power on the enemy before me.

"You've clearly trained," Saoirse said, knocking me out of my reverie.

I turned away from the door, breath held. Had I been that obvious? "I don't know what you mean."

"You're super fit, even for a fae, and your skill is the sword." She started moving further down the hallway, and I fell into step beside her. "Obviously, you've practiced, even if you've had to do it on your own."

"Oh." I relaxed. "It's honestly one of my favourite things to do. It's why I'm gutted to be assigned cleaning duty."

Saoirse gave me a conspiratorial smile. "King Lugh would love to have another warrior on the team. He won't be planning to keep you on cleaning duty forever. You just have to prove yourself first."

I stopped short in the hallway, frowning. "But how? I thought that was the entire part of the trial."

"The trial was meant to test how badly you want to join us here, which you did brilliantly." She grabbed my arm and pulled me along the hallway. "Come on. Everyone is waiting."

When Saoirse said *everyone*, she hadn't been joking. We stepped into the Great Hall, transformed overnight. The twenty wooden tables were gone. In their place were throngs of fae dressed for a night out at the clubs. Coloured balls of light hung from the timber roof-beams, swaying back and forth on an invisible breeze. Musicians crowded on the dais around the throne, closing their eyes as they played their instruments.

I braced myself as we stepped into the middle of the crowd. The Court had thrown this party to welcome me, and I wasn't exactly the most extraverted fae in the world. I liked to swing my sword, but I wasn't a big fan of small talk.

But as Saoirse led me through the crowded party, Celtic music swirling through the air, not a single pair of eyes turned my way. No one said hello. I didn't even get a scowl.

Huh. Well, in that case, it was time to take advantage of the little freedom I finally had. Back in my room, I'd found some paper in a drawer, and I'd written a note for Clark. I just needed to find a way to get outside, only for a brief moment.

"I'm going to take a look around," I half-shouted to Saoirse over the din of laughter, chatter, and music.

She gave me a nod and a thumbs up, and then drifted toward a group of fae wearing nothing more than silk nighties.

I decided to head in the opposite direction. A long wooden table pushed up against the wall had caught my eye. Food was piled on top of it. Pastries and pies, cakes and blocks of cheese. Wine bottles sat waiting for me to pour. My stomach grumbled.

Not now. I needed to get this note to Clark, and then I could return to the party to binge on carbs. I glanced around, my eyes landing on a door in the far corner. Bingo. That was it.

I hurried through the crowd, casting one last glance over my shoulder to make sure I wasn't being watched.

No one was looking at me at all. I might be the guest of honour, but I clearly wasn't welcome here. Not yet anyway. With a deep breath, I pushed open the door and stepped outside.

Much to my disappointment, there wasn't much out here. Instead of escaping into the courtyard, I'd stepped onto a balcony overlooking the plunging cliffs. The city below glowed with light, but a thick mist obscured the sparkle.

I let out a low whistle, one I'd practiced many times.

A moment later, a pair of dark wings rushed by my head. The raven settled on the wrought-iron railing, its beady little eyes staring deep into my soul. Clark had a connection with these birds. They would do her every bidding. And it had been waiting for my call.

I slipped the tiny scroll into the raven's outstretched claw. It simply read, *I'm in*.

Due to the blood contract, I couldn't say any more than that for now.

The raven blinked, and then soared into the sky.

As I dropped back my head to watch it disappear into the mist, the door behind me swung wide. "What are you doing out here?"

My heart skipped a beat. It was Lugh.

Steadying my breathing, I turned to face him. "I was trying to find the toilet."

He pursed his lips and stepped closer. "Do you often find yourself lost on your way to the loo?"

As if time itself had slowed, I barely breathed. Surely he didn't recognise me from that night at the Pack headquarters. Right? He had only seen me for a fleeting moment, and I'd looked completely different then.

If he knew I'd been there, he never would have let me inside of his Court.

He'd know I wasn't who I said I was.

He'd know I was lying, either then or now.

Probably both.

"Fortunately, no," I finally said. "Your castle is very large. It's easy to get lost."

He wrapped his strong hand around mine and motioned at the door. "The dancing has begun, and you're missing it."

"That's okay," I said. "I'm not really much of a—oh!"

Lugh kicked open the door and yanked me back inside the Great Hall with a kind of intensity that snapped all the words out of my mouth. He had a vice-like grip on my hand, and he propelled me straight past the tables full of food and drink.

"What the hell are you doing?" I snapped, trying—and failing—to yank my wrist away.

"It is customary for new members of this Court to dance during their welcome party."

With that, he yanked me onto the dance floor and wound his arm up my back. Hot lava poured through my veins as I tipped back my head to glare up at him. Celtic music swirled through the air, and the fae surrounding us took a step back. Lugh spun me across the floor, his feet moving in time with an ancient fae dance.

"You look delicious," he growled.

A thrill went through me. I couldn't help it, even as angry as I was. My new plan was starting to work. Seduce the king. Learn his secrets. And then somehow get the information back to his rival.

He spun me across the floor, our bodies moving

in sync. His lips brushed against my ear. "Where did you learn to dance like this?"

My mouth went dry. I'd been so caught up in the moment that I hadn't stopped to think. A solitary fae wouldn't know these dances. She would have never stepped foot in a fae ball before.

I pulled back and gave him a demure smile. "How many times do I have to tell you that I like to do my research?"

"And yet, your research turned up nothing about me." He spun me around in a circle, and then pulled me tight against his chest. I lost my breath, just for a second. But only because he'd been tossing me around like a ship at sea, not because of anything else.

"Should it have?" I squeaked out as he began to dip me low to the ground. I clung on tight, my fingernails digging into the skin behind his neck. "You said you've kept your existence a secret. You're a wraith."

"If you look hard enough, you can find me." He yanked me up against his chest again, and then ran his hand down the length of my back. My entire body went tight. Heat flooded my veins.

And then the music stopped.

As suddenly as he'd swept me into his arms, Lugh stepped away. He gave a slight inclination of his head. "Enjoy your party."

Mouth open, I watched him leave. What the hell had that been? My hands clenched, and I stalked after him. He couldn't just walk away. Not after that. We'd been in the middle of a conversation. Granted, he'd practically been speaking in riddles but still. It had felt like I was growing closer to some sort of realisation about the king, and then he'd vanished into the throngs of partygoers.

I stopped and cast my gaze around the room. Ah, there he was. Pushing out of the Great Hall's doors toward the courtyard. I hurried after him, determined to finish our conversation. As far as I knew, I'd be locked in my room all day again tomorrow, only to come out when a floor needed to be swept. This might be the last time I could speak to him for awhile.

When I pushed out into the courtyard, I sucked in a deep lungful of fresh, misty air. The room had been clogged with fae. Heat had seeped into my skin. The cool Edinburgh night was soothing after that.

I cast a glance around. The courtyard was quiet and empty. Cobblestone ran underfoot, and tall stone walls loomed all around. In the center stood a bronze statue of a male atop of a horse. The features had long since been worn over the centuries, but the sharply-pointed ears and javelin in his hand made it clear this male had been a warrior fae like me.

And Lugh was nowhere to be seen.

With a frustrated sigh, I zoomed across the courtyard. There was a high level arch overhead connecting The Royal Palace to the building next door, and I headed straight for it. When I reached the arch, I continued on, and rounded the next corner.

There he was. Hidden in the darkness with two other shadowy forms. Adrenaline tripped in my veins as I pressed my back against the stone wall before they could spot me. What, pray tell, was the king doing lurking around in the shadowy alley?

I slowed my breathing and flicked my hearing toward their conversation.

"Anderson's been in touch. He has a lead on the cauldron," the voice said—female, soft, and scared.

"Good," Lugh murmured. "Did he mention where he thinks it is?"

"He didn't want to give that information over the phone," the other shadow said. This one was male, nasally, and high-pitched. "Said his line has been tapped before."

"Good," Lugh said. "We do *not* want anyone to find this cauldron before we do."

My heart thumped. It was that damn cauldron again.

What cauldron? Just say what bloody cauldron it is!

"What are you going to do when he finds it?" the female hissed. "You can't just keep it here at Castle Wraith, not when—"

"You leave that part to me," Lugh interjected. "Eoin, I need you to keep searching the books. Find anything you can that will help expedite this."

Lugh stepped back and turned my way.

My heart leapt. Cursing silently, I scrambled back out into the courtyard and high-tailed it across the cobblestones. I reached the door heading back into the Great Hall at the precise moment that Lugh stepped out from beneath the arch that spanned the two buildings. His eyes settled on me, and I paused. His stride remained steady; his expression never wavered. I wanted to wrench open the door and storm inside, but that would look far more suspicious than if I stood here with a shit-eating grin on my face.

Maybe.

When he reached me, he wrapped his hand around where mine grasped the brass handle. "Enjoy your midnight stroll in the courtyard, Moira?"

His voice was full of ice. Nervously, I wet my lips.

"It's hot in there," I said in a garbled voice. "I wanted some fresh air."

"Some fresh air now. A loo before. But really it's an earful, I imagine." He cut a sharp glance my way. "I've been patient with your prickly personality, but I don't appreciate being spied on."

A shiver went down my spine, but I forced myself to remain still. "I said I wanted fresh air, and I did. It's not my fault you were lurking in the shadows having secret meetings."

"I'm the King of this Court. I can have secret

meetings wherever I damn well please," he growled. "The fact that you don't seem to understand or respect that makes me question your reasons for being here."

Narrowing my eyes, I wrenched my hand out from under his. "Maybe you'd understand my reasons better if you didn't lock me in my room all day!"

His lips curled into a wicked smile. "Oh, you didn't like that? Good. You can stay in there twice as long tomorrow."

6

*L*ugh hadn't been lying. The next day, he woke me up at six again by pounding on the door. It didn't matter that the entire Court had been up until four partying. *I* had to be up and at 'em, according to him. And he'd threatened to keep hammering on the wall if I tried to go back to sleep.

Despite waking at the crack of dawn, I was locked in my room until noon, at which point I was chaperoned over to the kitchen to clean up after lunch by a bushy-haired fae named Selma. Once I'd swept up every last crumb, I was hastily returned to my room. That continued for the rest of the day. And then the next. I'd get bustled out of my room to clean, have zero chance to speak to anyone, and then I had to go straight back.

The only fae who seemed to have any interest in getting to know me was Saoirse. She popped in to see me a few times a day and to smuggle in contra-band like chocolate and pizza.

"You doing okay?" She quietly shut the door behind her.

"No," I said glumly. "I am really tired of watching Tipping Point reruns. I now know every answer to every pub quiz question that ever was."

She wrinkled her nose. "I'll admit this sucks. I'm loyal to King Lugh, but...if I'm honest, I think he's taking your trial period a tad too far."

I gave her a look. "My trial period should have been surviving a load of Sluagh."

"I'm sure he'll come around soon," she insisted. "He's just had a lot on his mind lately."

I sat up a little straighter. "Like what?"

Sighing, Saoirse popped a pizza box on the desk. The tempting aroma of pepperoni and cheese swirled into my nose, and my stomach grumbled. "You know I can't tell you that. Anyway, I'll try to talk to him. I might be able to convince him to give you more freedom in the castle."

Any freedom would be more freedom than this.

"Thanks, Saoirse."

"Don't thank me too much." She pointed at the pizza. "You better hurry up and eat that now. I'm here to collect you for your favourite thing in the entire world."

"Cleaning duty," I muttered. And then I dug into the pizza like it would vanish without a trace if it sat waiting for even a second longer.

~

Saoirse dropped me off in what I'd started referring to as the "servant" quarters. It was a tiny room at the far end of the residential building where the crew gathered before the daily cleaning duties. Inside, it held all of our supplies as well as a whiteboard, where everyone's names and tasks were listed. So far, I'd only seen it in passing. I'd merely been told what to do and moved on.

The bushy-haired fae who had been dispensing the tasks now stood before the whiteboard with her hair tied up in a frizzy bun. She tapped the whiteboard with a red marker. "We've got a busy day ahead. There's only twenty of us and three hundred of them."

I glanced around the room, wondering how these fae had ended up here. They couldn't all be newbies.

"First order of business. The king's out on his weekly visit to town," Selma continued as she scribbled on the board. "Time for his room clean. Any volunteers?"

A few murmurs spread through the room, but there weren't any takers.

I edged forward. "I'll do it."

I couldn't believe my luck. This was the perfect opportunity to get back on track with my spying mission. There must be something inside Lugh's room that could clue me in on what he had planned. Papers lying around. Rubbish he'd tossed in the bin. Big flashing neon signs he'd hung on the walls...

Selma snorted and slid the cap back on the whiteboard pen. "Absolutely not."

I crossed my arms. "Why is that? Because I'm new? I think I'm capable of making a bed, thank you very much, regardless of whose arse sleeps in it."

A murmur went through the cleaning crew.

Wicked amusement flickered in Selma's eyes. "Alright then. Think you're up to the task? Go 'head. Clean the king's rooms. Imogen here will go with you."

Imogen towered over me at around six feet tall. She had bright pink hair, a nose piercing, and a swirling tattoo on her stomach, shown off by the cropped tank top she wore with black skinny jeans.

We both opened our mouths to argue. Me because I couldn't very well snoop through Lugh's stuff if I had someone watching my every move. And Imogen because, well...it seemed like the entire cleaning crew was pretty averse to the idea of tidying up the king's rooms.

"Nope!" Selma stopped us before we could get in a word. "Moira, you wanted to do it, so you're getting what you asked for. Imogen, you can't keep avoiding this task for the rest of your life. Now, go. Shoo. Get on with it, the both of you."

With a grumble in my direction, Imogen led me

over to the cupboard full of cleaning supplies. We loaded up with bin bags, cleaning rags, and a hoover, and made the trek over to the Royal Palace. It was a commanding building inside the same square where the Great Hall had been built. In the middle, a small tower rose up above the flat roof, holding an ancient clock with golden arms.

We entered a small wooden door beneath an oversized wrought-iron lamp. Inside, Imogen led me down the red-carpeted floor to a grand arched door at the end of the hallway.

"You've gotten us into it now." Imogen balanced the bucket of cleaning supplies in her arms, and then kicked the door open. We strode inside, and I came to a sudden stop. The place was an absolute tip.

"What the hell?" I squeaked.

"Yep." She tossed me a bin bag. "Welcome to the wonderful task of cleaning up after Lugh. He's a great king, but..."

I bit back the urge to contradict her and gazed at the mess. "How long has it been since you last cleaned it?"

"A week. He always goes into town on Thursday mornings, and we like to clean it when he's not around to watch. It makes him grumpy."

I gawked. I couldn't help it. Lugh's living quarters were made up of three open-plan rooms. The living area stretched out just before us where two dominating sofas formed a V around a twenty gallon aquarium. The floors were beautiful, glistening hardwood, from what I could see, but every square meter hid beneath piles and piles of books. There were books on the sofas, books on the coffee table, and books sitting on top of lampshades.

If it hadn't been so messy, I would have been impressed. The lofted white ceiling was carved in intricate, antique designs and the wood-panelled walls were just as elaborate. Bronze candle-holders were scattered throughout, and the center stone fireplace took my breath away. It was big enough to fit an entire car inside of it. Above a mantlepiece, a golden horse and a silver lion held up a coat of arms between them. That same sigil was on it—the cloaked figure hidden in the mist.

I inched further into the room and looked to the right where Lugh's bedroom hid under...more books. The ivory sheets were on the floor, along with his pillows. Pens and pieces of parchment decorated the walls as if they'd been taped there haphazardly.

To the left was the kitchen, but no meals were cooked there.

It just held more books.

"Any idea what this is all about?"

Imogen was already busying herself. She'd made a stack of books by the archway separating the bedroom and the living room, and she seemed to be placing them into colour-coded piles.

"He's researching," she said firmly as her pink

hair fell into her face. "Most of these books are hundreds of years old."

"I can see that," I coughed. The dust was as plentiful as the books.

Imogen stood and pointed toward the sofa. "Come on then. You were the one who wanted to clean his room. We start by sorting the books and stacking them in piles by the walls. We need to clear the floors and furniture, so we can give the place a good clean."

With a shake of my head, I got started. While Imogen focused on the living area, I headed into his bedroom to take a look around. She was right. Even if I wanted to snoop, there'd be nothing to see unless we cleared all this away.

As I grabbed the books from his bed, something caught my attention out of the corner of my eye. It was a glistening oak case tall enough to brush the top of the ceiling. I stepped back, surveying it with interest.

The case held a spear. Next to it sat a black shield with a hard boss of white bronze. It was a pretty basic looking shield, but the spear...

I took a step closer. It was one of the most beautiful weapons I'd ever seen. With its five points, it could do some serious damage. The heads were a dark bronze, each one tapering to fine and very sharp points. They were all fastened to a rowan shaft and latched into place by gleaming golden rivets. But the most interesting part about this spear wasn't the craft of it. It was the magic seeping out of the case.

It looked nothing like the spear from the Sluagh vaults. That had only had one tip, and it had been silver, not bronze.

But what were the odds? I wouldn't really call a spear a typical weapon of choice. Curious, I reached toward the handle.

"You can't touch that!" Imogen leapt toward me, her eyes wide and fearful. She grabbed my hand and yanked me away from the case.

"Whoa, calm down," I sputtered. "I was just taking a look."

She held up her hands, shaking her head as she stood firmly between me and the case. "You can *not* touch Lugh's spear."

I narrowed my eyes, but I nodded anyway. "Yeah. Okay, got it. I didn't know."

"Not even the case," she warned.

"Yep. Not even the case."

She gave an uneasy nod and then moved away before turning to get one more warning in. "It's locked, by the way. You wouldn't be able to open it, even if you wanted to. Just...don't try."

"Okay," I whispered, watching her trembling back as she rejoined the pile of books on the living room floor. As soon as her focus was off me, I risked another glance at the case, heart pounding.

Despite being a beautiful spear, I couldn't imagine what about it could inspire so much terror.

It reeked of magic, but it was locked away, so it wasn't like it could actually get to us out here.

I flicked my eyes toward Imogen and then back at the spear. "So, what's the deal with this thing? Why do we have to stay away from the spear?"

Imogen glanced up, her pink hair falling into her eyes. "Because if you touch it, you'll burst into flames."

I blinked at her. Okay, I hadn't expected that. "Say what now?"

She let out a little giggle. "I'm just kidding. I don't actually know why we can't touch it."

"So then....what about all that....?" I waved my hands, referring to her frantic freak-out.

Her expression sobered. "Lugh doesn't want us near it, but I don't know why. All I know is he'll punish anyone who tries to even open the case. And his punishments are far worse than the trials. He tends to do it in secret, but...we've all heard the stories." She inclined her head toward my broom. "If I were you, I'd forget about the spear and start cleaning. Now."

$\mathcal{E}$yebrows furrowed, I paced from one end of my chilly room to the other. Lugh had a spear, one he was terrified for people to touch. The person who had helped me in the vaults had also wielded a spear. The two could very well be linked.

Lugh could have been the one to help me in the vaults, even if it made no sense at all.

That fact alone would mean bonus points for Lugh. But I'd also just found out that he liked to chop off people's hands.

It had been a few days since I'd last seen him. My little mission to seduce the information out of him wasn't going exactly as planned. I needed to ramp things up a notch and fast, or the cauldron would be in his hands before I even knew what it did.

When the cleaning tasks were being assigned the next day, I quickly stepped in to cover the training room. I'd found nothing of note in Lugh's room, though I hadn't been able to search his drawers or his cupboards yet. Unfortunately, his room wouldn't come back into rotation for another week, so I needed to try a different approach.

"I know a lot about handling and cleaning weapons," I interjected before Selma could even finish listing the options for the day. "I'm happy to take on the training room."

Selma slid her eyes toward Imogen. "How'd she do with the king's room?"

"Fine." Imogen shrugged. "Bit complain-y about the mess, but aren't we all?"

Selma flashed me a wicked grin. "Bet you won't be se eager to clean his room next week, now will you?"

I decided to hide that I was in fact *very* eager, as I didn't want to raise any suspicion. Knowing her, she was probably far more likely to send me back again if she thought I didn't want to do it. "I didn't know that it would be like that."

Selma snorted. "The king is one of a kind. Very well. You put in the time there. You can have the training room today. Imogen, you'll go with her again."

Imogen didn't complain this time. Instead, she shot me a wink and a thumbs up. My heart raced in excitement. It felt like years since I'd stepped foot inside a training room, even if it had been a week at most. I knew I wouldn't have a chance to train now, but I wanted to walk inside the space, breathe in the scent of it.

And I wanted to see if they had any spears.

We grabbed the cleaning supplies and headed to the training room. I pushed open the door but stopped short when I saw who was inside. Imogen slammed into my back, but the impact didn't nudge me forward. My head felt fuzzy. All the blood in my veins began to boil.

Lugh spun across the blue training mat like a tornado. He had a silver-tipped spear in his hand, and he whirled it sideways like it was an extension of his arm. He jabbed it forward at an invisible foe and roared. The invisible foe stood no chance against a charge like that.

Sweat glistened on his exposed back muscles. His midnight blue curls hung in his hooded eyes. As he continued through his next set of moves, I couldn't do anything other than stare.

"Oh right. I forgot. We need to wait outside," Imogen muttered, grabbing my arm to pull me back.

I pulled out of her grip and stepped further inside the training room. The door slammed shut behind me, booming through the cavernous space.

Lugh's elaborate routine came to a sudden stop. He twisted toward me and scowled.

I held up my bucket. "Sorry. Came here for a clean."

Why the hell was I apologising? I ought to be

shouting at him for making me mop up after him in the first place.

"You're meant to check the log books before bursting in here with your mop and bucket." He snapped the spear into its stand against the wall and stalked away from me. "You interrupted my training session."

"A pretty impressive training session at that," I said, following close behind.

He stopped suddenly but kept his glistening, toned back turned my way. "Has my hearing failed me?" As I inched around him, I caught a glimmer in the corner of his eye. "That sounded like a compliment."

"Maybe because it was one." I edged a little closer, coming to a stop when we stood face-to-face. "You're good with a spear."

His lips quirked. "Of course I am. I'm the best in this Court. Perhaps the best fae alive."

Bloody hell, this male was cocky.

Feigning disinterest, I leaned against the wall while I watched him towel the sweat off his body. It was difficult to stay focused, but I had a mission. "Anyone else in the Court good with a spear? I've only ever met sword fighters."

He slowed, towel pausing between the dip in his abs. "Most fae prefer the sword, but I'm curious how you've met so many warriors."

Dammit. Not again. I kept forgetting to down-play my knowledge about the fae.

"There are more solitary fae out there than you think." Was that even true? Didn't matter. All that mattered was convincing Lugh it was true.

"Now *that* does not surprise me." He dropped the towel into a wicker basket in the corner and grabbed a stainless steel water bottle. As he took a long chug, I couldn't help but notice how a few drips escaped and ran down his chin, and then neck, and then chest...

Ahem.

"You talked about signing in," I tried. "Do you have a weapon's log as well? Something that people have to sign when they take them out of here?"

Lugh stopped chugging and gave me a suspicious glare. "If you're thinking of taking a weapon out of this room, then you are going to be very disappointed."

"Mostly, I'd like my own weapon back, thanks," I snapped.

Narrowing his eyes, Lugh leaned forward and wrapped his hand around the back of my neck. All logical thought fled from my brain. My heart barely worked. A beat here, a beat there. Not that I even noticed. The only thing in the world that existed was his hot as fire touch against my skin.

I swallowed hard.

"You will get your weapon back when I decide that I trust you."

"And when will that be?" I whispered.

His eyes dropped to my lips, and he frowned. "Fate is certainly a strange beast."

My heart skipped another beat. "You're speaking in riddles again."

"I'm not speaking in riddles, and you know it." With that, he dropped his hand and pulled away. "Your cleaning friend is outside, listening to every word we say. I should let you two get on with your job."

Lugh took another chug of his water, and then strode toward the training room doors. Frustrated, I called after him. "Are you the only fae in this castle who fights with a silver-tipped spear? If so, then I have a riddle for you. One that involves the—"

With a growl, he whipped toward me. "Do not question your king."

He ripped open the door to reveal a wide-eyed Imogen creeping in the background. Without a single glance in her direction, he stormed down the hallway and disappeared from view.

Imogen's mouth dropped open. She pointed at the king, and then at me. "You two are..."

"We are nothing," I hissed. I knew how this probably looked to her. Like some kind of lover's quarrel.

"Have you slept with him?" she whispered.

I scoffed. "No. Of course not. I barely even know him. Besides, he's not my type."

My type definitely did not involve cocky arse-holes with perfect midnight hair, gorgeous cheekbones, and back muscles that were something straight out of Greek God artwork.

Imogen didn't look convinced, and I didn't want to hear anymore. I grabbed the mop and bucket, and got to work. But the feel of his skin on my neck was much harder to drown out. I could still feel where his fingers had touched me, like they'd left behind an impression, a mark.

I needed to get a grip.

~

"Saoirse, we need to talk."

My new friend froze halfway through the doorframe. Her purple eyes furtively cast for an answer to my sudden demand, darting from one corner of my room to the next.

"What's happening?" she finally asked, though she made no move to slither further inside.

I flicked my eyes to the hallway behind her. Several fae passed by. A green-haired female slowed to eavesdrop on our conversation. With all the enhanced hearing flying around this place, the only way to have a private conversation was with the door firmly shut.

"Come inside," I insisted. "I don't want anyone listening."

She pondered my request for a moment, but then hurried inside. When the door was finally shut,

I spilled out my words. "The night of my trial, there was someone else in the vaults."

She pressed her lips together, crossed the room, and peered out the tiny window at the cliffs below. Nothing about her expression screamed surprise. So, Saoirse already knew. Another point in the Lugh column.

"Are you going to say anything?" I asked.

She turned to face me. "This isn't a conversation that I can have with you. You need to ask the king."

"I tried," I said plaintively. "But he refuses to talk about it."

"Then I'm afraid I can't help you." She let out a tiny sigh, crossed the room again, and peered out the tiny peephole in the door. Then she turned to face me. "Look, all you need to know is that not everyone in this Court can be trusted."

I cocked my head. Well, that was certainly the last direction I'd expected this conversation to take. I'd dragged her in here wanting to know answers about Lugh's spear, and instead we were talking about something else...and I didn't quite understand what that *something else* was just yet.

I furrowed my brows. "What are you talking about?"

Her purple eyes slid to the door. "It's hard to hide things in a place like this."

"Because of the..." I tapped my ears.

She nodded. "We have protective wards on the doors, but they don't block out everything."

"Are you trying to say that someone is listening to our conversation right now?" I asked in a harsh whisper.

"Maybe." She shrugged, seeming far more at ease about this whole thing than I felt. Sure, I'd used my own enhanced hearing to my advantage many times before, but suddenly it felt like my every move was being watched. And I didn't like it. "The thing is, we can't know every time someone is listening. So it's best to keep mum."

Mum about the spear. And mum about the vaults.

Suddenly, life in this Court started to make a lot more sense. Everyone had a furtive look about them. No one spoke of things out loud. There were meaningful glances everywhere but never meaningful words. It was hard to imagine why until now. Not everything was sunshine and roses in the Court of Wraiths. There were traitors amongst the traitors, and they didn't know who they were.

"Can we talk somewhere else?" I asked. There was so much I needed to know, and it seemed like Saoirse was willing to tell me—as long as there was no risk we'd be overheard.

"There's only one place in the castle that cannot be breached by fae ears," she said in a low, meaningful voice.

My stomach dropped. "The vaults."

She laughed. "You should see the look on your

face. No, I don't mean the vaults, though they'd work in a pinch. I meant The Royal Palace."

"Oh, for fuck's sake," I muttered. "What are the odds?"

"No odds. He picked the palace for his living quarters for that very reason, as did all the masters and royals before him." She clenched my arm and lowered her voice. "It's the only place in the castle where he can..."

"Where he can what?" I asked, breathless.

Her eyes flashed with something. I knew she was trying to communicate with me without words, but we still hardly knew each other. I didn't understand what she was trying to say at all.

"Read his books."

8

A new day and a new mission. I was once again going to talk my way into Lugh's room and rifle through his books. There were answers in the millions of pages he had in there, though I had no idea where to start looking.

But when it came time for our daily assignments, Selma was insistent that King Lugh's quarters did not need cleaning until the next Thursday. It had only been two days, and his head might explode if we stacked his books again already.

Instead, Imogen and I were assigned to tackle the large stretch of garden that backed up onto the western defences. They were high stone battlements that stretched around the castle's edge, looking out over a sheer cliff. Even in January, the grass needed to be clipped and weeds had to be yanked out of the soft ground.

Just behind us were two more buildings that

formed a square, earlier residential quarters that were no longer in use. Saoirse had told me in hushed whispers that the buildings had been abandoned since the witch trials. Humans in search of magical culprits had stormed the castle and set the buildings ablaze. Fae had been trapped inside, and no one had wanted to rebuild the place, not even Lugh.

Instead, he'd left the square as it was, as a memorial, and had named it Mag Mell.

I was surprised to learn he was that sensitive.

"Can I ask you a question?" I asked Imogen as I blew a stray strand of hair out of my face. "How'd you end up here in the Court of Wraiths?"

Imogen stiffened, but then kept on pulling weeds. "The king likes to collect strays."

I leaned back on my heels and cocked a brow. "Strays?"

"Yeah, like you. Solitaries." She shook her head and tossed a weed onto the growing pile. "Or runaways, fae fleeing from abuse, criminals, and those with useless gifts."

"Criminals?" I asked, startled, even though I shouldn't have been. Of course Lugh welcomed them into his Court. It was just the kind of thing he'd do. Hell, I was halfway convinced he was engaged in criminal activity himself.

"*Former* criminals, for the most part," she corrected. "Like me. I was a thief. Humans were mostly my targets, but I stole from fae, too. I even had a wanted poster with my photo on it back in Glasgow. I had to leave to get the heat off me."

"And Lugh gave you a place to stay."

"Me and a bunch of others. I think he believes we can be rehabilitated." She chuckled. "I don't actually agree with him on that, you know? I haven't been able to completely stop. Why do you think I'm part of the cleaning crew? I can't be trusted with something more important, like guarding the castle or taking care of out-of-control vampires in the city."

Wiping the sweat off my brow, I regarded Imogen carefully. This had given me some food for thought, and I didn't know whether it was the good kind of food, like pizza, or the bad, like rotting meat. Lugh took in the unwanted, or at least the fae who felt they weren't wanted. That was kind of sweet. But a bunch of dangerous criminals under one roof had the potential to create a pretty toxic environment. Imogen was only a thief, but what kind of crimes did the others have under their belts?

Were there any murderers? I shuddered.

When we were done, my hands were bright green and in desperate need of a wash. I headed straight back to my room, eager to get back inside for the first time since I'd arrived here. Saoirse caught me along the way, falling into step beside me and looking about five million times more put together than I was.

I had yet to determine what her role here was in

the Court of Wraiths. Her gift was a mystery, and there was something different about the magic that pulsed around her. She read as fae to me, but also something else, something I couldn't quite put my finger on...

"How are you settling in?" She nodded toward my hands. "Looks like you've had a busy day."

"Garden duty," I said. "Better than washing dishes but not as good as swinging steel."

"You think any more about what I mentioned yesterday?"

She was referring to her hint about Lugh, no doubt. Truth be told, I'd spent a lot of time thinking about her little puzzle, mostly when I'd been ripping weeds out of the ground. It had been therapeutic in a way. There's nothing quite like destroying things to make your life seem less full of suck. But I hadn't gotten anywhere on her hint.

"No," I admitted, coming to a stop outside my bedroom door. "Can you maybe be less cryptic?"

She thought for a moment. "Maybe. I might be able to give you..."

Saoirse trailed off when I opened my door. My room was trashed.

"Blimey," Saoirse whispered. "Stay here. I'll be back in a mo."

I edged into the room while she vanished down the hallway. Shattered glass covered the ripped rug. The bedsheets had been sliced in half, and the old, sagging mattress had been ripped to shreds. Even some of the floorboards had been pried open to reveal a cold empty darkness below.

Shivering, I took a step toward the hole and peered down. I couldn't see a damn thing. If a Sluagh hand reached up right now...

"Moira?" King Lugh sauntered inside. He took one look around the room and whisked me into his arms. I yelped as he carried me out into the hallway and deposited me into a heap on the floor. Pain lanced through my bum. And then he slammed the door behind him. An unexpected concern flickered across his features.

I blinked up at him, dazed. "Are you serious right now? You can't just yank me into your arms and then throw me onto the floor! I know you're the king of this castle, but I—"

A muffled *pffffft* echoed from inside the room. Blue smoke drifted out through the cracks around the door. Lugh reached down, launched me to my feet, and dragged me even further down the hallway. Everyone else who happened to witness Lugh's startled reaction followed suit, rushing away from the mysterious cloud.

"Hmm." Saoirse shot Lugh a frown when we were a safe distance away from the blue smoke. "That I didn't see coming."

I shook my arms until I was free of Lugh's grip. "Is someone going to explain to me what the hell is going on?"

"It seems that someone doesn't like you," Lugh

said dryly, his cocky boredom quickly replacing whatever concern I'd thought I'd seen in his expression.

"No shit," I said with narrowed eyes. "It doesn't take a puff of blue smoke for me to figure that out."

"It's not blue smoke," Saoirse whispered. "It's a sorcerer's potion. I've seen it before. It's supposed to make you..." She cleared her throat. "*Pliable*."

I scrunched my eyebrows. "Pliable?"

Lugh coughed, and I could have sworn his sharp cheekbones looked just a tad more on the pink side than they normally did. "It's called Sapphire. Consider it the magical equivalent of the human ecstasy drug, although it seems to heighten libido even more than it does."

"Oh." My own cheeks got hot. "Who the hell would put a magical libido potion in my bedroom?"

Probably not a question I wanted answered, if I were being honest. A secret admirer, trying to catch me unaware? Not that I really thought I had one of those inside the castle. Only a few fae had even bothered to talk to me, much less try to woo me into bed. Or maybe it had been the hobgoblin. This was exactly the type of trick they liked to pull.

"The heightened libido isn't the focus, in this case," Lugh answered. "Whoever left this here only wanted to make you pliable."

"You sound really sure of that."

"This isn't the first time it's happened," Saoirse

added. "There's, ah..." And then she clamped her mouth shut.

"We should all leave this hallway before the vapours reach us." Lugh turned to Saoirse, speaking over my head as if I weren't even there. "We'll need to move Moira out of this room and into another. Let's cordon this one off for the foreseeable future. And we'll need to burn the sheets, and her clothes. Otherwise, the magic will be impossible to get rid of."

"Um, hi," I said, raising a single finger. "No burning my clothes, please. I only have a couple extra shirts with me, and I would prefer not to walk around naked."

"You can borrow something of mine for now," Saoirse said. "Let's get you to your new room, and I'll find something for you to wear."

My new room sat on the very top floor, where the heating system had failed months ago. There was a tiny electric radiator in one corner, but it did little to warm the space. Other than that, it was almost exactly the same as the other room. Same bed, similar blankets, and a very threadbare rug that matched.

Saoirse gave me an apologetic smile. "Unfortunately, we don't have any open rooms on the floors below, but I'll see what I can do about finding you somewhere warmer soon."

"I don't mind. Honestly." I stopped her just before she turned to go. "Saoirse, what's the real deal about that smoke bomb? You said it's happened before."

She nodded, nibbling on her bottom lip. "Yeah, and that's why you don't have to worry. It wasn't really aimed at you. Several other fae have been hit with it, including me."

I arched a brow. "*You* got hit with it?"

"Yeah, I'm close with Lugh, and..." She shook her head. "What I can say out loud is that there are rumours going around that you and Lugh are..." Her cheeks went red as she cleared her throat. "You know. Involved."

Bloody Imogen. We were going to have to have a chat later.

"We're not involved," I said quickly.

"Oh, I know that," Saoirse piped. "But not everyone else will."

Ah. I understood what she meant now. Some of the fae would believe the rumours and think I had some kind of 'in' with the king. That I would have knowledge or access, and they would be able to get to him through me, because that bomb would make me pliable.

So Saoirse hadn't been wrong when she'd warned me earlier. Not everyone in this castle could be trusted.

That included me.

~

*I*t had been a few days since I'd checked in with Clark, and I'd come up with a plan to get some information into her lap. All I needed were a few moments alone outside to find her raven. It would no doubt be searching the skies, waiting for a moment it could approach me.

Luckily, everyone was so distracted by the smoke bomb that they didn't notice me sneaking out of my upstairs room. Saoirse had forgotten to lock it for once. She probably felt sorry for me. A twinge of guilt went through me. I was using her empathy to my advantage, which didn't feel great...well, I'd just have to brush it aside for now.

In my drawer, I'd found another notebook and pen. I wasn't able to write down anything useful, but I'd come up with a system of numbers. Numbers that should mean something to Clark. She might be confused at first, but I was certain she'd figure it out.

I pushed the door open and dashed across the cobblestone courtyard. The raven perched on the tip of the horse statue's long snout. The paper rippled in my fingers. I was glad the bird was out here, waiting for me. It wouldn't take long for someone to notice I'd gone missing.

A dark shadow loomed from behind the statue. Heart constricting, I slowed to a stop, suddenly realising how very alone I was out here. My sword had been stowed away somewhere inside of the castle, out of my reach. If the fae behind the smoke bomb had followed me out here...

When the moonlight splashed onto the lurker's face, I gasped. Lugh stepped out of the shadows, his entire form hidden beneath a long black cloak. He strode toward me, the heavy fabric rustling against the cobblestones.

"I thought I might find you out here, yet I hoped I wouldn't," he said in a low growl.

Unease flickered through me, but I squared my shoulders. "What's the big deal? I'm tired of being locked up in my room, and I want some fresh air."

He narrowed his eyes as his cloak fluttered in the light wind. For a split second, I could see inside the folds. He didn't have a spear. Thank the Morrigan. Not that I actually thought he would use it against me. Now, more than ever, I was convinced he'd been the one in the vaults.

Why had he helped me fight the Sluagh? Who the hell knew. This male was a hard one to figure out. It was clear he didn't want me dead, though. Not yet, at least.

"You were rushing around like you have somewhere to be, not like you wanted a leisurely evening stroll," he pointed out. "What's that in your hand?"

Bollocks. The note for Clark. I crumpled the paper and wound my hands around my back. "I don't know what you mean."

"Give that to me." He closed the space between us and wrapped his arms around my back, digging his fingers into my wrists. A flutter went through my stomach as his body pressed tight against mine. Electrifying magic shot through my veins. I gasped when he kept me close, wrenching my hand toward his eyes.

I still had a fistful of parchment.

"A note. To whom?" Without another word, he nipped at my hand. A tremor went through me at the feel of his mouth on my skin, and instinctively, my grip on the paper loosened. An evil grin stretched across his face, and he took the note from my fingers with his teeth.

"I thought that might work," he murmured.

I swallowed hard, my eyes locked on where his lips pressed against the sheet of paper, like a strange kiss.

Slowly, he stepped back and extracted the note from his mouth. All I could do was watch, eagerly drinking in his every move. There was something so...otherworldly about him. His movements were fluid and strong. Everything about him screamed power and confidence. If this male had a weakness, I certainly couldn't see what it was.

Other than he was an arsehole traitor, of course. Couldn't forget about that...

He frowned as his eyes tripped across the parchment. "What *is* this? What do these numbers mean?"

I tried to bite back a smile. The blood contract might be a pain in my arse, but at least it had kept him from discovering the truth about why I was here.

"Sizes," I chirped. "Since you had to destroy all my clothes, I wanted to go shopping in town. Unfortunately, a very controlling king caught me on my way."

"You said you wanted fresh air." His eyes narrowed. "And you needed to write down your own sizes in order to buy yourself some clothes?"

"These are Saoirse's sizes," I lied, hoping he wouldn't have a clue about female clothes and the fact she was an entire dress size smaller than I was. "We aren't exactly the same size and the clothes she lent me are a little tight. I thought I'd grab something for her, too. As a thanks. For being the only fae in this castle who seems to give a damn about me."

He let out a frustrated sigh and ran a hand through his hair. "I can see we haven't been particularly welcoming to you, have we?"

I barked out a laugh, more from surprise that he'd actually asked than because of the question itself. "Seriously? You forced me to do a dangerous trial, one that could have killed me. You locked me up in a room for hours on end without anyone else to talk to. You practically threw a broom at me instead of letting me train what I'm good at—fighting with my sword. And then someone bombed my room, for who knows what reason. Do you think that's welcoming?"

The words rushed out of me like an avalanche

of thoughts, feelings, and emotions. I hadn't meant to speak so plainly. I hadn't even realised how frustrated I was. This was a spying mission, after all. Who cared if these fae wanted to have anything to do with me? Who cared if this false king hated me or not?

I certainly didn't. Not even a little bit.

"I see."

Was that his only response? I crossed my arms and glared at him.

"You need some clothes." He handed me the crumpled parchment. "Only a few shops will be open this late. I'll accompany you down the hill to the Royal Mile."

I got a double dose of relief and frustration. Sure, I was glad he'd bought my story, but I was getting sick and tired of being chaperoned everywhere I went. Plus, I hadn't actually meant to go into town for clothes tonight at all. I wanted to get my note to the raven and return to my snooping duties inside the castle. "Is that really necessary?"

"Yes," he said emphatically. "You will either accept my company into town, or you can go back to your room for the rest of the night. You got your fresh air. Best stay inside where it's safe."

I propped my fists on my hips. Damn him. I didn't actually care about the clothes. Saoirse had lent me enough that could stretch to fit me, and Lugh was right. It was late. The options were pretty limited, especially on the Royal Mile, which was filled with tourist shops. With a heavy sigh, I glanced back at the castle buildings and then toward the looming gate outside of the square. I couldn't bear another long night locked up in a room with nothing but the television to keep me company.

Besides, maybe I could prod him for some information.

"Yeah, alright," I grumbled. "You can come along. Just don't expect to join me in any changing rooms."

He flashed me a wicked grin. "If I wanted to get you naked, I wouldn't need to trap you in a changing room."

My mouth parted; my heart skipped a beat. Where the hell had that come from?

Chuckling, he motioned me toward the gate. "That was a joke, Moira. You always seem so tense, so serious about everything."

I fell into step beside him. "That's pretty rich coming from you. You're like...like the *king* of being over-serious."

"Oh, we're doing puns now, are we?" He pulled a set of ancient rusted keys from his cloak and unlocked the gate door.

"That a problem?" I snipped. "You can make jokes about getting me naked, but I can't use puns?"

"On the contrary. All jokes are welcome. The *Moira*, the merrier." He sniggered.

"Oh god. That was terrible." But, somehow, I still found myself laughing.

We pushed through the gates, and I blew hot breath on my hands as Lugh locked up behind us. It was chilly in Edinburgh when the sun vanished from the sky. That ever-present mist cloaked everything, hiding even the gleaming streetlights in the glum.

"You're not from around here, are you?" Lugh asked as we began our descent into the city. "Your accent. It isn't Scottish."

"No," I admitted. "As I'm sure you can tell, I'm English."

Some people were good at putting on accents, but I wasn't. One of the first things I'd decided about this mission was that being as close to *me* as possible was the best way to make it as a spy. Fewer things to fake. Fewer lies to remember.

He cut his eyes my way. "When did you move to Edinburgh?"

"Oh, about five days ago," I said with a laugh, but I had to check his face for a reaction. Hopefully, my confession wouldn't transform him back into that closed-off, suspicious king he liked to be so often. Somehow, it seemed like I'd broken down at least a section of the wall he had erected between himself and the world. I didn't want him to throw the bricks at my face.

"Ah." He nodded. "So you really did come seeking us out."

"Seeking *House Athaira* out," I corrected. "I had no idea at all that things had changed."

He considered my words for a moment. "And are you disappointed by what you found instead?"

"I..." Hmph. How was I supposed to answer that? He seemed to be under the strange impression that his Court was some kind of utopia. "Have you already forgotten all that stuff I said? About not feeling welcome?"

"Unfortunately, no," he grunted.

We fell into uncomfortable silence after that. It was impossible to talk to Lugh without one of us winding the other up, or both. He wanted me to love his Court of Wraiths. I wanted him to see how much it sucked arse. We were never going to agree. About anything.

We passed through the wide open space of the Castle Esplanade, where hundreds of sorcerers—and wrongfully-accused innocent humans—had been burned at the stake during the witch trials of the 15th century. Ancient stone buildings rose on either side of us as the cobblestones returned beneath our feet. The trek down Castle Hill would lead to the shops and pubs, where we would hopefully find something open for business.

The streets were empty and dark. January wasn't a popular time for locals or even tourists, who'd rather stay beside the fire in a pub, downing pints of Guinness to warm the gut. I risked a glance at Lugh when the moonlight slipped through the cracks between two buildings. His outline was fierce, sharply cut, and towering in an otherworldly sort of way. Power pulsed from deep within him with every step he took.

Who was this fae? And why had I never heard of him?

He was blatantly powerful. He commanded respect and inspired confidence from hundreds of fae, some of whom had placed trust in Athaira before him...who was...where exactly? I had so many questions and so few answers. This male beside me had them all. With his head held high and that strength rolling off his toned body...I could see why the Scottish fae wanted to believe he could be king.

"I can tell you want to ask me something," he murmured as we passed by an old church, its steeple disappearing high into the darkness above.

I took a deep breath and decided to broach the one subject I'd been dying to tackle, above all others. "You were in the vaults the night of the trial. And you helped me."

His footsteps faltered, and he almost imperceptibly shot a quick glance over his shoulder. "That's an interesting theory."

"You don't seem at all surprised that someone was down there with me," I countered.

He waved his hand in dismissal, though I saw his jaw clench. "You must have mentioned it to Saoirse. She tells me everything."

"Uh uh." I wagged my finger at him. "She refuses to talk about it. Something about the fact that you can't say anything in the castle without someone else hearing it."

He raked his hand through his hair. "You mustn't repeat this to anyone."

My heart skipped a beat. Was he actually going to open up and give me some answers? I wanted to fist pump the sky.

"Okay," I said eagerly.

"I did help you," he admitted. "Saoirse is part Druid. I asked her to read your future, as I always do before trials. The number of Sluagh in the vaults has...multiplied, without my knowing. If you had gone in there alone, you would not have won your trial."

I came to a sudden stop on the cobblestones. My eyes were wide as I stared at him, and my heart felt as if it had been twisted like a snake. I'd only met one Druid in my life before this. Caer, who had the power to look into the future and dispense prophecies to whomever she pleased.

I'd heard a prophecy from her once before, one I wished I could forget.

And now this...

"So, you're saying I *actually* would have died?" I whispered. That single word echoed in my ear. *Died, died, died.* I wanted to block it out, but I couldn't. My death had been on the cards. I'd been so close to the end of my life, and I hadn't even known it.

"Not due to your lack of skill or strength," he quickly countered. "There were far too many in there for one fae to fight alone. I merely took a few out of the equation for you. That was why I instructed you to go to your right. I tackled the tunnels on the left side."

This was too much. I needed to sit down.

"Why the hell didn't you just call off the trial?" I hissed. "Why make me go through with it, if you knew I was going to *actually die*?"

He pressed his lips together, and his eyes darkened. "There are things you don't know, things I cannot tell you. Even here, away from ears that always listen. Just know that I could not stop the trial without risking everything."

"Everything?" My fisted hands shook by my sides. "So, I guess *my life* is okay to risk but not all these other mysterious things you refuse to tell me."

"Moira." He growled and grabbed my shoulder. "You're not listening to me. I was there, in the vaults, to make sure you didn't die. I was never going to let death get anywhere near you. That's why I had Saoirse do the reading. Hate me for keeping secrets, but don't hate me for risking your life, because I never did. And I never would."

My heart trembled as I stared into his inky eyes. "Oh."

He let go of my shoulder and resumed the walk down Castle Hill. The change was so abrupt that I didn't know what to make of it. We'd been arguing, he'd been so fierce in his words, and then he'd just started walking again like nothing at all had happened.

With a deep breath, I followed behind.

He cast a glance over his shoulder. "I don't know if Saoirse warned you, but you shouldn't talk about anything private inside the castle."

"She told me." I picked up the pace to catch up with him. "She also said that your room was the only place where conversations couldn't be overheard."

"That's right." He rubbed at his light-stubbled jaw. "Something Athaira's predecessor put into place around the Royal Palace, but I haven't been able to replicate it anywhere else inside the castle."

I was tempted to prod him for more information about Athaira, but I could tell by the shuttered look on his face that he was done with secret-spilling for the night. Instead, I would have to take a different approach.

"You asked me when I moved to Edinburgh. When did you?"

"I have lived here all my life." There was something in his voice that caught me off guard. A sorrow, one that echoed of deep, long-held pain. It was an easy question and a simple answer, but the way he clipped his words betrayed him. There was more to it than that.

"And you were part of House Athaira...?" I knew I'd asked the wrong question as soon as his shoulders tensed.

"No," he growled. "Enough about me. Tell me about your sword. Where did you get it?"

I gave myself a moment to think as we passed another church and swung a right into Parliament Square, away from the Royal Mile shops. We crossed the square, darkness hugging us close.

I frowned. "Where are we going?"

"Shortcut," he replied, leading us beneath a series of stone archways. "Tell me about your sword."

"A friend gave it to me." I cast a glance around. We'd somehow ended up on a thin close—the Scottish word for alleyway. The cobblestone ground was steep and snaked between the rear of buildings. Bins were stacked up beside back doors, rotting rubbish spilling over the sides. It stank of dead fish. The wrought-iron street-lamps flickered in the dark. An unease whistled through me.

Lugh latched onto my arm and pulled me to the left, toward a flight of stairs that led down into the dark.

"Um," was all I could muster.

"There's a clothing shop down this close that caters specifically to supernaturals," he said briskly. "It shuts in twenty minutes."

His voice held zero room for disagreement, but I didn't like how this night had suddenly taken a turn for the worse. With the King of the Wraiths dragging me down a dark alley and demanding to know more about my sword. A sword that I conspicuously did not have at the moment.

"Honestly, stop. I don't want to go any further into this creepy alley with you." I dug my heels into the cobblestones. "Let go of me now."

He growled and shoved me against the stone wall, pressing his body tightly against mine. My breath hitched. Leaning down, he pressed his lips to my ear and breathed.

"Don't say anything. We're being followed."

9

My brain fogged on his words, my mind too distracted by his electrifying touch. Then, slowly, the meaning sank in, and I dropped my voice to a low whisper. "You serious?"

He gave a solemn nod.

I glanced around us. "That's why you brought us here? Wouldn't it have been better to stay on the busy—"

He slid his hand over my mouth to shut me up. Narrowing my eyes, I growled and tried to nip at his skin.

"Someone has been trying to sabotage the Court for months." He mouthed the words, and strangely, I could understand what he was trying to say. That meant he thought they were fae. The magical Sapphire drug. The silence in Saoirse's words. It was all connected. And now the culprits had followed us down the Royal Mile.

Lugh mouthed his next words. "This is my chance to stop them."

I decided not to point out that both of us were regrettably unarmed. He didn't have a spear, and I certainly didn't have a sword, since *he'd hidden it from me*. If we were being stalked by traitorous arseholes who wanted to tear him from his throne, then we would need a lot more than two pairs of fists.

Lugh took a step back, his eyes flashing with a kind of ferocity he hadn't yet shown me. I'd seen a range of expressions from him so far: boredom, cockiness, concern, amusement, and wickedness. But now he looked hellbent and fierce. I kind of liked it.

Too bad he didn't have a spear.

"You stay here," he mouthed, taking another step back and pointing down the close in the direction of the way we'd come.

My eyes widened in realisation. He hadn't brought us here to hide in wait for an attack. He'd brought us here so he could dump me next to the bins. Lugh wanted to go fight the stalkers by himself.

I shook my head and pointed at his cloak, where there was a glaringly obvious lack of a spear. Then I pointed at myself and mimed holding a sword before me. I was trying to remind him that I was a warrior. I was trained to fight, even if I didn't have my weapon of choice. I didn't need a sword to put up a good fight. But Lugh didn't know that. He thought I was a solitary fae who'd spent her entire life on her own, without access to coaches and training facilities.

"I'm your king," he hissed softly. Then he walked away and rounded the corner.

For a moment, all I could do was stare after him. He was risking his life, a second time, to keep me from getting hurt. I hadn't expected that from him. He was the King of Wraiths. He'd formed a secret Court, hidden from the rest of the fae world. He'd seemed so callous and uncaring. At first.

But that was because he *was*, I reminded myself. I had seen him at the Pack headquarters, with my own two eyes, asking for a cauldron that would help him steal the crown from Clark.

I was here to stop him. I was here as a spy, not as one of his subjects. He wouldn't be so eager to help me if he knew the truth.

My heart beat hard at the distant echo of his footsteps on the cobblestone. He suddenly stopped, and several more footsteps sounded through the close. Whoever had been following us now surrounded Lugh.

My heart lurched as a deafening silence filled the air.

He may have ordered me to stay here, but I wasn't *actually* his subject, so I could do whatever I damn well pleased. Besides, maybe I could finally get some answers. Everything that had happened so far seemed linked. So it only stood to reason that whatever Lugh had planned with the cauldron could have something to do with why these fae were trying to take him down.

Yeah. So helping him would be helping me. *Not him.*

At that, I gave myself a nod and pushed away from the stone wall. Creeping down the close, I kept my footsteps silent. I couldn't afford for them to hear me coming, not unless I wanted to be dragged out of the shadows and exposed for what I really was: a spy.

I followed the twists and bends until I came to a small square at the end of the close. Lugh stood in the center, surrounded by about a dozen armed fae. With a sharp gasp, I ducked into a doorway and peered around the side.

The fae were all clad in black, and their faces were obscured by hoods. I could only tell what they were by the way they held their bodies, the grace in their tiny movements, the magic that rippled like sound waves around their limbs. Every supernatural has a certain *feel* about them, and I could always recognise a fae.

Lugh crossed his arms over his chest, his black cloak billowing around his feet. "Ten of you. That's more than I thought."

One of the fae answered by cracking his knuckles.

"Is no one going to speak?" Lugh asked smoothly, his face transformed by that cruel apathy he'd shown me from the very first day. I was starting to realise that Lugh only looked bored when he was anything but. "At least tell me *why* you wish to kill me."

One fae strode forward from the rest. A tall, large female with a voice that sounded like rain on the wind. "We know who you are, and we appreciate your heritage. But we also know you've been searching for the cauldron. Why, Lugh?"

Lugh squinted at the fae, but his expression showed no recognition. "You must be mistaken."

The female tsked. "A liar, too. That can only mean one thing. You're searching for the cauldron to stop us from bringing back your creator."

Frowning, I cocked my head. *Bring back his creator?*

Lugh's entire body went stiff, and his voice dropped to a growl. "Don't speak of her."

The fae let out a little laugh and drew a gold-edged sword from her back. "You and your constant 'don't speak of this' and 'don't speak of that.' So paranoid. It must be a terrible way to live, hiding everything from everyone. I guess that means we'll be doing you a favour. Just think of it like this. We're putting you out of your misery."

My eyes flicked from Lugh's stone-cold face to the warriors drawing their weapons. He was completely surrounded with no spear to keep him company. I didn't need to be a druid to know how this fight would end.

The female swung her sword at Lugh's head. He

dropped low to the ground, grunting as he rolled to the left. The female scrabbled toward him. She slashed her blade toward his head, but he shifted left just in time, and the steel rang as it hit the stone ground.

Gritting my teeth, I cast my gaze around me for anything that would help. I spotted a metal sign, displaying a flat for rent in the building above. Not ideal, but it would do. I yanked it off the wall and charged.

The warrior nearest me didn't see me coming. I slammed the sign into the back of his head, and he crumpled to the ground without a word. But that was pretty much it for the element of surprise. I'd caught the attention of the others now, and they were all staring at me with bulging eyes. I couldn't see the rest of their faces, hidden by their black masks.

Except Lugh. He just looked furious.

"Moira," he growled. "Get out of here. *Now*."

I spun the sign in my hand and shrugged. "Nope. I owe you one."

The female fae whirled on her feet to face me. Her entire face was obscured by a black cloth. Not even her eyes were visible. Damn. She must be someone that Lugh knew. From the castle, perhaps? Maybe I'd met her, too. All I had to go on was her voice, which I didn't recognise, but that was easy enough to change. A little warble here, a low growl there. Easy peasy.

Her laughter echoed through the close. "The new recruit. What do you think you're going to do with that sign, love?"

Ugh, I hated it when people called me 'love' in such a patronising tone.

"Lots of things. First, I think I'll slam it against that pretty little head of yours," I snapped.

Her sword trembled in her hands, and it was my turn to laugh. She was getting blinding mad. Good. The madder I got 'em, the more mistakes they'd make.

"Your choice," she hissed before turning to face her fellow traitors. "Kill the king. Don't spare the girl."

With that, everyone sprang into motion.

Another attacker rushed toward me, sword held high. Before he could reach me, I hurled the sign at his head. It smacked right into his face, knocking him to the ground. As he fell, I reached for his sword, but it seemed to vanish into thin air, along with the guy I'd just hit.

Bollocks. They had some sort of sorcerer spell to get them out of here fast.

I didn't know what Lugh was doing, but I didn't dare look. The next warrior was running toward me.

Skidding across the cobblestones, I flew toward the sign and grabbed it from the ground. But I didn't make it in time. The warrior reached me first.

He wrapped his hand around my shirt and yanked me away from the sign.

But that meant he couldn't use his sword. I whirled on him and slammed my fist right into his nose. He let go, giving me just enough time to grab my sign again. I shoved it right into his already bleeding nose and watched him crumple to the ground.

Three down...seven to go?

I turned to see Lugh had three more fallen fae around his feet, vanishing into the nothingness, but the female was bearing down on him. She'd slashed him with her sword, and blood oozed out of several wounds on his arms and chest.

With my sign held tight in my hands, I thundered across the close. But before I could reach Lugh, two pairs of hands latched onto me. They grabbed my arms and yanked me back, while another snatched away my sign.

Chest heaving, I ripped out of their grip. The three fae closed in around me. They were unarmed. So far. They'd been too busy grabbing me to unsheathe their swords. One held my new favourite weapon of choice—the sign—but he tossed it across the alley before I could try to get it back for myself.

It fell with a clatter. Up above us, I heard the unmistakable sound of gasps as the humans peered out their windows at the fight below.

Great. Human onlookers, probably scared out

of their ever-loving minds. That was definitely going to help the situation.

I bounced on my toes. "You lot just going to stand there staring at me?"

"No." They drew their swords in unison.

10

Okay, so this wasn't ideal. I'd taken on multiple enemies more times than I could count, but never without a sword. They all had weapons, and they'd been ordered to take me down, dead or alive.

So I did the only thing that anyone else would do when faced with impending death: I turned tail and ran.

My feet pounded the cobblestones as I raced away from the attackers. They did exactly what I wanted them to do and chased after me. When they stormed my way, I took a sharp turn right and jogged back to where they'd discarded my sign.

Grinning, I snatched it from the ground and held it before me. Sometimes, brawn really isn't the way to win.

When they saw I had the sign once again, two of the attackers forked away and headed toward

Lugh to help their leader. Dammit. I'd been trying to draw them away. He had deep slashes all over his skin, and his blood painted the ground. As strong as he seemed, I could tell the wounds had slowed him down. His feet stumbled as he ducked beneath another blow.

But my attention got dragged away from Lugh when one of my opponents lobbed spit at my boots. "That sign isn't going to help you forever, love."

My eyes narrowed. "Oh yeah? Then, why don't you come here and try to fight me, *love*?"

It was kind of an empty threat, one my opponents were more than happy to call me on. They both rushed toward me, their heavy boots clomping hard on the stone. Gritting my teeth, I held the sign before me as their blades clashed hard.

The force of their blows knocked me back. I slammed onto the ground, my teeth knocking together.

Before they could rush me, I jumped to my feet with my enhanced fae speed. I whirled the sign toward them, catching it on one of their swords. The weapon ripped out of his hands and skittered across the cobblestones.

I looked at his sword.

He looked at his sword.

And then we both dove.

My shoulder hit the ground hard, and my fingers wrapped around the hilt of the weapon. Instantly, magic sang in my veins, lighting up my every nerve. New power swirling through my gut, I tossed the sign to the side and stood.

I grinned and held up the sword. Every single fae in the close turned my way, even Lugh. "Oi, you wankers. Why don't you try fighting me now?"

The prat whose sword I stole stumbled away and disappeared around the bend. I turned toward the one who had spat on my shoes. His expression was hidden beneath the black mask, but I could see his eyes. Unease churned through his green irises.

The female—who I assumed was some kind of leader—and two of the remaining fae made steps toward me.

I motioned with one hand toward the nearest attacker, and he took the bait. He sprang toward me. Without even thinking, I knocked my blade against his, ducked low, and then swung my sword at his leg.

My weapon made contact, slicing right through his skin. He yowled, his scream echoing through the silent night. He crumpled to the ground, his face twisted in pain.

"Bollocks," the female muttered. She held her ground and motioned for the other two fighters to rush toward me.

I risked a glance at Lugh. He'd fallen to his knees. Blood poured from his stomach wound. He needed help. And soon. Or this entire fight would be for nothing.

But there was no time to think about that. I met

the two attackers head on. One managed a swing. I ducked down and rolled to the side. He hacked his sword at my head, but it rang against the stone instead. I jumped back to my feet and levelled my gaze.

He threw his weight behind his sword and sailed it sideways toward me, just as his buddy did the same. Drawing the magic of the sword in through my veins, I moved. My blade knocked against his, and it clattered from his hands. I swung fast and met the other. The force of my blow knocked him back.

They both stared at me, jaws agape.

"She wasn't lying. Her skill is the sword," the female muttered, casting a glance over her shoulder at Lugh, whose hands were splayed against his bleeding wound. "Let's go now. He won't survive that."

As they grabbed their wounded friend, I tightened my grip on the sword. The itch to fight burned through me like fire. I couldn't just let them walk away from this.

But then Lugh's groan cut through my thoughts. I twisted toward him and winced. He was in bad shape. If I went after the attackers, there was no way he'd survive. With one last look at the black-clad fae rushing out of the alley, I shook my head and jogged toward Lugh instead.

He was a lot heavier than he looked. I hauled him to his feet and faltered on the cobblestones as I attempted to drag him down the long, winding close.

"Don't try to go to the castle. Go back to that place I took you," he hissed. "I wasn't lying. Safe...supernaturals."

I frowned. Go back to that place? Did he mean the end of the alley where he'd left me? Fine with me. Dragging him all the way up Castle Hill would have taken five million years, but I could probably get him to the other end of the close before he bled out completely. Gritting my teeth, I wrapped one arm around his waist and stumbled in the right direction.

The heat of his body melted against me as we walked. His hand tightened on my shoulder; his fingers dug deep into my skin. I wet my lips and continued on, ignoring the rush of magic storming through my veins.

When we stumbled into the shadows at the end of the close, I glanced around for some kind of answer. He'd mentioned a shop before, but I didn't see one along the dimly lit alley. All the windows were completely dark, save for one.

"Lugh?"

His eyes were shut; his breathing was shallow. Dammit. He'd passed out, and I had no idea where to take him. Grunting, I slid him off my body so that I could peer into the glowing window. It was dark inside, save for a single lamp that flickered in the back corner. It sat next to a tiny little shield propped on a table. On it was Lugh's sigil.

I'd never been so relieved to see that creepy hooded figure.

But how the hell would I get inside? Frowning, I glanced down at Lugh. He'd had a ring of keys before. I knelt beside him and dug through his pockets, trying not to think about how close my hands were to certain…*things*. Heat swirled through my veins, and I tried to shake wayward thoughts out of my mind.

Ah, there they were! I grabbed the keys and held them up before me. One of these would do the trick. After trying several, I finally found the right key. The door swung open, and I grabbed Lugh beneath his armpits and dragged him inside.

I glanced around. Now what? The living room I'd found myself in was pretty basic. A two-seater sofa, a small coffee table with marble coasters, an old telly with an antenna perched on the top. There were no decorations, no picture frames of smiling faces. This was some kind of safe house.

There might be a first aid kit somewhere, but as I stared at Lugh's wound, I had a sinking suspicion that it would do no good. Nothing about the cut on his stomach was normal. It oozed blood in a frantic kind of way, like it was desperate to get out of his body. There'd been something magical about that attack, and a few bandages would do nothing to save him.

We needed some help here, and I wasn't sure where to find it.

Shaking my head, I strode out of the room and found myself in a kitchen. Nothing much to see there, either, other than a phone and a printed list of numbers that was attached to the fridge by a magnet.

I ripped the paper off the fridge and dialled the first number.

A few moments later, an alarmed voice crackled through the receiver. "Who is this? What's wrong? What's happening?"

My shoulders sagged in relief. I knew that voice. "Saoirse, is that you?"

"Huh?" A moment passed. "Wait. *Moira?* Why are you using the safe house phone? Wait. Are you okay?"

Thank the Morrigan it had been Saoirse who'd answered the phone. If it had been anyone else, I might have had trouble explaining what had happened.

"I'm here with Lugh. We got attacked in Barrie's Close, and he's...not in great shape. He's bleeding everywhere, and he's completely unconscious."

"The king is hurt?!" Her whispered voice rushed through the phone. "Wait, he was attacked? Did anyone touch his spear?"

I frowned at the question. Why would that matter? "No, we were unarmed, which is how they got us." Edging back toward the door, I glanced into the living room where I'd left Lugh passed out on the floor—I hadn't been able to lift him onto the sofa. "Listen, he's in really bad shape, and I'm not a healer. What should I do?"

"There's a kit in the bathroom in the cupboard above the sink," she said quickly. "Apply the salve to his wound and put one of the bandages around it."

"Um." I frowned at the gash on his stomach. "It's a big-ass wound, Saoirse."

"Then use his shirt. Just get it covered until we get there."

The phone clicked in my ear. I held it away from me and stared before slamming it back on the wall. My heart thumped as I took another glance at Lugh. Help was on the way, but I hoped it wouldn't be long. The colour had begun to drain from his face. I didn't want to think too hard about what that meant.

Scurrying into the bathroom, I found the cupboard and the kit inside. It had that same sigil etched onto the front, which was a good sign I'd found the right thing. When I returned to the living room, I dropped to Lugh's side and grabbed a glass medicine bottle clearly labeled, "Salve."

When I unscrewed the top, I had to wrinkle my nose. Blimey, this shit stank like rotten eggs mixed with burnt plastic. Whatever this was, it was potent, which hopefully meant it would do the trick.

I spread some across my hand, grimaced, and

then dabbed it against Lugh's wound. Blood smeared onto my hand. Scrunching my nose, I continued dabbing the salve until I'd covered everything.

The whole room reeked now, but it was done. I grabbed Lugh's shirt and ripped off a strip of it, revealing more of his chiseled abs. Swallowing hard, I pressed the cloth against the wound, sat back on my heels, and waited.

I'd done what I'd been told, but I didn't think it was enough.

Lugh hadn't even flinched, and his chest barely moved as he breathed.

He was dying, and for some bizarre reason I didn't understand, the very core of me—my soul—felt scared.

11

Saoirse burst through the door, her dark hair floating around her shoulders as if she'd just been hit by a lightning bolt. Her eyes swirled around the room before landing on Lugh's unconscious form spread across the floor. Her body tensed, then relaxed. She twisted toward the door and flicked her fingers.

Several more supernaturals strode into the little hideaway. Two more fae, the ginger-haired warriors from the night of my trial, whose names I'd since learned were Warin and Boudica. They were twins.

A sorcerer edged into the safe room behind them. I sniffed, narrowing my eyes. I wasn't a big fan of sorcerers. Every time I went near one, something terrible tended to happen. They sucked in drama wherever they went, like some kind of tornado of problems.

I was pretty sure they liked it that way.

This guy, though, reminded me nothing of the sorcerers I'd met before. He was built like a tank, his hair buzzed short. It highlighted his thick neck covered in elaborate tattoos. Dark ink crept up the side of his face to his hairline. I drank in his clothes. He wore dark jeans ripped at the knees, black boots, and a heavy metal band t-shirt.

Sorcerers—unlike fae, vampires, and werewolves —were human. They just happened to be gifted with magical abilities from the power that had seeped into this realm from the fae realm. It didn't run in bloodlines, and it didn't matter where you lived. It just showed up, unexpectedly. Many sorcerers spent their entire lives never knowing what they were, just thinking they were freaks.

"Axel," Saoirse said, waving emphatically at the sorcerer. "Take care of Lugh's wound. You two," she said as she swivelled toward the warriors, "keep a look out in the close, just in case the attackers come back."

"I don't think they're coming back," I said quietly. "They got what they came for."

"We can't be too careful," she said in a snap.

"Hey now." I held up my hands. "Don't take this out on me. I'm only repeating what one of the attackers said. They wanted to take Lugh out, and they did."

Her expression softened. "I'm sorry. I'm just

worried. He hardly ever leaves the castle without a spear, and so I've never seen him like this before."

She was scared, worried for him, just like I'd been. It was inexplicable for me, since I kind of hated the guy. He was a traitor and a cocky arsehole who was making my life miserable. I shouldn't have cared. I'd been wracking my brain while I'd waited for the others to arrive. Why had I fought so hard? Why had I gotten his literal blood on my hands trying to save his life?

It didn't make any sense. And yet, when I looked at him wounded on the floor, I felt that twinge deep down inside of me again. The urge to help. The desperation to keep him alive.

Maybe that was his power. Maybe it wasn't skill with a spear at all.

Maybe he was able to command unwavering loyalty and devotion in his subjects. It would explain why he'd made his own court.

"Axel, what are you thinking?" Saoirse asked the sorcerer, who had knelt beside Lugh to examine his wounds.

The sorcerer gave her a grim smile. "Unfortunately, Moira was right to be concerned. The weapon that cut him was doused in magic. It's preventing him from healing, so there's no way to stop the blood or close the wound."

My heart hammered against my ribcage. "So you can't fix him?"

"Oh, I can fix him," Axel grunted. "I can

counter the magic with something of my own, so that he can begin to heal normally. But if you hadn't called me in..."

I glanced at Saoirse whose face had gone pale.

"Right," she whispered. "Do what you can for him, please."

"And I'll get my payment?"

"Of course." Her eyes flashed as she stared down at him. "Have we ever not paid you?"

He shrugged. "Nope, but I have to check. I've been stiffed by others enough lately that I can never be too sure."

Interesting. So this sorcerer took on a lot of work. "Did someone happen to hire you to make a blue smoke bomb thingy lately?"

He cocked his head in confusion.

"Sapphire," Saoirse added. "Moira got hit with one."

He grumbled. "No, I don't touch that shite. You're probably looking at Jezebel for that kind of thing."

Jezebel? Arching my brow, I turned back to Saoirse. If we could track down the sorcerer creating the smoke bombs, maybe she could lead us to the traitor inside the court.

Wait a minute. What was I thinking? I wasn't here to *help* the Court of Wraiths. I was here to take them down.

Who cared who made the damn Sapphire when

that mysterious cauldron was out there, waiting to take down my queen?

Saoirse gave a quick shake of her head. "We already looked into that. Jezebel loves making Sapphire, but she'd never sell to a fae. She hates us."

With that, Axel snapped open a leather bag he'd brought along with him and extracted a grimoire. "Worry about your Sapphire problems later. I need to get to work."

While the sorcerer did his thing to Lugh's wounds, Saoirse dragged me down the hallway so that we could have some privacy. "Tell me what happened."

Deciding not to go into detail about the whole clothing situation—particularly since I'd made up a few white lies involving her, I explained that Lugh and I had taken a field trip into town. Eventually, he'd noticed someone tracking us. Everything became a whirlwind after that.

"I couldn't see their faces," I explained. "All of them were wearing cloaks and hoods and masks. One of them was a female fae. I think she was the leader. The others were male, I think. Not all of them spoke, so it was hard to tell."

Saoirse frowned. "You disobeyed his orders?"

Bollocks. Maybe I should have left out that part. It was going to come back to bite me in the ass, wasn't it?

"I'm a warrior at heart," I tried with a shrug. "Sometimes, my urge to fight takes over."

She cocked her head. "So you rushed in to help him fight these ten traitors."

"I guess," I said warily. "The important thing here is, who were they? Lugh didn't seem surprised to see them. He even mentioned something about—"

Saoirse pressed a finger to my lips. "Just in case."

I flicked my eyes down the hallway. The sorcerer wouldn't be able to hear us, but the fae might if they were really keen to listen in. But they were part of the warrior team.

"Wait a minute," I hissed. "You really think...?" I jerked my head down the hall, to indicate the two warriors keeping watch in the close.

A second later, Saoirse whisked her phone from her back pocket and typed a note. She flashed the screen my way.

Someone on the inside is working against us. We can't be too careful.

Frowning, I grabbed her phone and typed my own response.

If you suspect one of them, why not take them off the warrior team?

Sighing, she rolled her eyes and took back her phone. Another message.

We have no proof either one is involved in anything.

"Everything okay back there?" Axel called down the hallway.

Saoirse tapped delete on her words and slid her

phone out of view. Conversation over. At least I finally had one answer, though it didn't really help *my* mission much. At the end of the day, whatever Warin and Boudica wanted to do to Lugh didn't matter when the king himself was plotting to tear down *my* Court.

Hell, maybe I'd been fighting on the wrong side tonight.

When we stepped back into the living room, the sorcerer was packing up his things, his impressive tattoos shining against the glow from the lamp. Lugh was still out of it, his expression peaceful for once. "The wound is closed now, so he's started to heal. Because of the magic involved, it might take him a little longer than usual to be back to his old self. Oh, and he's half-awake, but probably not for long." The sorcerer looked at me. "He was asking for you."

"Me?" I gargled.

Saoirse smirked. "I'll show Axel out and discuss with the others how to transport Lugh back to the castle safely. Be back in a moment."

She disappeared out the door before I could ask her to stay. Staring down at Lugh, I shifted on my feet. He didn't look awake. His breathing was steady, exposed chest rising and falling. The deep gash in his stomach still looked bruised and raw, but it no longer spilled a river of blood on his skin.

"You...aren't good...at following orders," he

wheezed, his eyes still closed. "I asked for you. Why haven't you come?"

Wetting my lips, I crossed the room and sank to his side. My knees dug into the hardwood floor. "You looked asleep. I didn't want to disturb you."

"You should not have helped me," he whispered. "They could have killed you."

Yes, they could have. And they tried as hard as they could. Without my sword, I'd been pretty vulnerable. At the time, it had seemed like the only possible choice. Help Lugh fight his attackers. Don't let him die by their hand. That strange desperation had churned through me, making me act without even thinking. But sitting on the other side of it now, I didn't quite understand why I'd fought for his life.

He was my enemy. I was here, in Edinburgh, to stop him from going up against my queen.

Now that he was safe and alive—even if a little worse for wear—that aching desperation inside of me had vanished, like the attackers into the night.

My heart felt as sore as my bruised muscles.

He cracked open his shadowy eyes and peered up at me. "You aren't going to say anything?"

"Sure. You're welcome," I snarked. "I accept rewards in the form of swords, training, and unlocked doors."

I didn't know how else to answer but to joke. Something needed to break the tension in the room, and this was all I had. I didn't like the way he was looking at me, like he was seeing me for the very first time, and he wasn't sure what he thought of the truth.

"Done." His eyes slid shut again.

"That's it?" I blinked down at him, wondering if I'd heard him right. "You aren't going to scold me for disobeying orders?"

And I was actually going to get some freedom? It was too good to be true.

"Oh, I will definitely dole out some punishment for your disobedience," he growled, a slight smile twisting up the corners of his lips. "But I'm waiting until I'm back at full strength for that."

A shiver went through me. In his state, I couldn't tell if he was joking or not. Probably more on the *not* side of things. Lugh didn't seem like the kind of king to take disobedience very lightly. That said, he was smiling. Was that because he enjoyed the idea of making me pay?

I shivered again.

Something to worry about later. Saoirse had opened the door again, and Lugh had fallen silent. He shut his eyes and sighed, and that strange ache tightened within me again. Even though the wound was closed and his healing had begun, he was in pain.

"We're taking an Uber up to the castle," Saoirse said in a matter-of-fact tone of voice. "It should be here in five. We need to get him ready."

"An Uber?" I asked incredulously, rising to my

feet. "Doesn't the king of a bloody Court have a fleet of cars?"

Clark certainly did. And a whole hidden garage that no one knew about, other than a few of her closest advisors like me. I suspected Lugh had the same. If he didn't, he needed to get on that, stat. Situations like this were precisely when secret transportation was necessary.

"If we send for a castle car, word will spread fast that something has happened to him. We can take him through the back gate. No one will ever know a thing."

Unless, of course, Warin or Boudica out there were the traitors Saoirse feared they might be. Most members of the Court of Wraiths might never find out, but the fae they wanted to keep the information from certainly would—the attackers who had tried to kill Lugh tonight. She seemed to sense my thoughts, pursing her lips.

"We have no other choice," she said.

"I'm just surprised there's a back gate," I tried, flicking my eyes at the door. If the warriors were the bad guys, I didn't want to tip them off that we were on to them.

"There's a hidden tunnel that goes up through the cliff and through the northern battery. No one knows about it but Lugh, me, and the warrior team. And even then, not everyone knows exactly where the entrance is."

And now me. I filed that information away for later use. That could come in handy.

A horn sounded outside. The taxi had arrived, and they must have offered double the rate, because the driver had reversed back into the close itself. Cars weren't typically allowed on these streets. Together, the four of us hauled Lugh to his feet and lifted him out the door and into the backseat of the car.

Saoirse turned to me and grasped my hands. "I'm sorry. There's only room for one more. Will you be okay getting back to the castle with Warin and Boudica?"

I understood what she was doing. Not everyone knew where the entrance to the hidden tunnels was, and she wanted to take Lugh through it alone. That meant Warin and Boudica were not in on the secret, and she wanted to keep it that way.

I squeezed her hands back and smiled. "I'll be fine. Those two will have my back, I'm sure."

She gave me an uneasy nod and slid into the front seat, waving goodbye. As soon as the car pulled out of the close, I started back to the castle with the warriors, my heart thumping with every step I took.

Even though no one had died here tonight, a heavy cloud of danger lurked over me. I still didn't understand the full truth of what was going on here, but I didn't need to. Whatever it was, it was pretty damn bad.

I'd fully stepped into the path of danger, and I was going to get hit by it if I didn't watch out. I glanced at the twin warriors. They were barely paying attention to me. This was my chance to leave, if I wanted.

But instead, I kept my feet turned in the direction of Castle Hill.

12

A knock sounded on my door. Groaning, I twisted in the sheets to peer at the clock, expecting it to be bloody six in the morning. I was surprised when the display said it was ten. Huh. That was a first.

It was also a little unnerving when the door didn't fly open and when the pounding didn't hammer its way into my brain. Instead, I had to slowly climb from the bed, pad across the cold floor, and crack open the door myself, blanket wrapped around my shoulders like a cape.

Lugh stood on the other side, looking a little worse for wear. His hair fell into eyes that were lined in red. His black shirt was rumpled, and he wore a loose pair of joggers, probably to keep his trousers from rubbing against the wound.

Still, the sight of him somehow pierced me to my very core.

"I'd like to speak with you," he said quietly. "Would you come to my quarters in half an hour?"

I arched a brow. Well...this was unexpected. "That sounds like a question. Not a command."

"That's because it *is* a question." He peered down at me, his eyes soft and searching for something in mine. "You can say no, but I hope you won't."

And with that, he spun on his heels and vanished down the hallway.

~

Obviously, I wasn't going to turn down a chance to speak privately with Lugh in a place where our words couldn't be overheard. Plus...his fancy case-enclosed spear would be there with him. Maybe I could finally get some answers about that...and all those books, too.

First, I had a stop to make.

The door to my room had been left unlocked, and no one was waiting in the hallway to chaperone me around the castle, which meant...maybe Lugh hadn't been delirious when he'd agreed to let me have a little more freedom.

Now that I'd saved his ass, he trusted me, at least a little more than he had before. Time to use that to my advantage and ignore the twinge of guilt in my heart because of it.

I owed him nothing. Not as long as he worked against my queen, my friend.

I still had the note full of numbers for Clark. If she could figure out my code, she'd learn that there was a new court in town, led by the traitor who wanted to find that mysterious cauldron. That was all I could manage to fit on the note in number form.

This time, I didn't risk heading into the court-yard. I bustled through the Great Hall, thankful for the quiet emptiness that filled the expansive space. It was between breakfast and lunch, and no fae roamed the rows of tables. Outside, on the balcony, I waited for the raven.

Clark would know what to do with this informa-tion. She'd always done the right thing before. I trusted she would do it again now. I hoped she would understand that the fae of this court were not all bad, even if some were. I barely knew them, but Saoirse and Imogen—even if she had a penchant for thievery—had proven to me that most of the fae here just wanted a safe, happy life.

At some point, if things continued like this, Clark would no doubt feel forced to bring her warriors here, to take up arms against the self-proclaimed King of the Wraiths. I just hoped no innocents got caught in the crossfire.

The raven finally spotted me and dropped onto the wrought-iron railing. With a shaky breath, I handed it the parchment and watched it soar away into the clouds. That was it then. If Clark could translate my code, she would understand what we were up against. And she would be waiting for my next note, the one that would tell her what Lugh planned to do to take her throne.

As I turned to go, a flash of red at the bottom of the cliffs caught my eye. Frowning, I leaned over the railing to peer down at it. Even with my fae sight, it was difficult to make out what it was. A vague figure. A person, human, fae, or otherwise. Someone with blazing red hair.

Warin, I couldn't help but think. Saoirse had mentioned a secret tunnel through the cliff, and he was down there now, looking for it.

Heart thumping, I pushed back into the Great Hall and headed toward Lugh's quarters. None of this concerned me, I tried to tell myself. Nothing I could say or do would make a difference.

I was more nervous than I had expected when I approached The Royal Palace. Last time I'd been here, Lugh hadn't been home and I'd had Imogen to keep me company. Now, it would just be me and him and the questions I longed to ask.

He opened the door before I knocked and motioned me inside. Swallowing hard, I followed him down the hallway and into the rooms he'd set up as his home. There were far more rooms than this inside The Royal Palace, but they were empty for now. For the first time, I couldn't help but wonder how lonely he was in here by himself.

"Sit." He motioned at the sofa, once again covered in books.

"Has anyone ever told you about these marvellous inventions called bookcases?" I said, smirking as I strolled through the mess. "They have shelves and everything. It helps keep these things from crowding the floor, your sofas, your bed."

He ran a tired hand down his face, but I swore I saw the glimmer of a smile. "Bookcases are permanent."

"And these aren't?" That surprised me. He obviously loved reading. Otherwise, he wouldn't have collected about a million different books.

He waved his hands at the stacks dismissively. "I cycle through the collections often enough that I don't want to get attached to how they look in my bedroom."

My heart slowed. What a strange way of putting it.

"You do mean your books, right?" I glanced around. "Or do you have visitors here often?"

And by visitors, I obviously meant...*visitors*.

The pain in his expression vanished, replaced now by a cocky ease. "If I did, no one would ever know." He leaned back, lacing his hands behind his head. "I could roar in pleasure as she screamed out my name, and not a single soul would hear but the two of us."

A tremor went through me, and a mental image sprang into my mind that I wasn't sure I would ever be able to shake. Lugh above me, nipping my ear and roaring in pleasure. My entire face felt as hot as the sun on the longest summer day.

Blimey, I needed to get a grip.

Clearing my throat, I settled into the armchair, picked up a book on the witch trials, and began to idly flip through it. "Why'd you call me in here, Lugh? I know it wasn't to discuss your fondness for cycling through books. And lovers."

He leaned back in the chair opposite mine, regarding me carefully. "You call me Lugh. Not your king."

Heat once again flooded my face. I hadn't even noticed. That was probably something I needed to stop if I wanted him to take me seriously.

"It's taking me some time to get used to using that kind of title," I said honestly. Even before Clark became Queen, it was always Prince or Master to the male who had been in charge of the Court. I hardly ever called *her* Queen now, either. It was just Clark. That was how we both liked it.

"Be careful," he warned. "I personally don't mind the relaxed approach to titles, but many here would consider it an insult to my authority."

I arched a brow. "Wait a minute. You actually don't mind? And here I thought most royals liked to insist on titles, particularly one who has kind of made himself his own king of his own made-up court. Respect and all that."

"I am not your normal king."

Something I was quickly realising myself. He wasn't like anyone I'd ever met, in fact. That said, I still had no idea what, exactly, he was like. Lugh was an enigma. A puzzle. One I was desperate to solve.

I snapped the book shut. "You still haven't told me why you asked me to come here."

He raked a hand through his hair and sighed. "I wanted to thank you for what you did last night. If you hadn't fought by my side, I might have died. If you hadn't called Saoirse, I could have bled out on the cobblestones. I owe you, Moira."

I shrugged, acting all nonchalant, but I couldn't ignore the frantic beating of my heart. "I was actually the one who owed you. For all the help in the vaults."

He gave a quick shake of his head. "I was the one who forced you to do the trial, so the help I gave you there did not create a debt that you owed."

I mean, he had a point...I was just surprised that he saw it that way, too.

I leaned forward and braced my elbows on my knees. "So what are you saying?"

His lips quirked. "I haven't forgotten what you asked for. A sword, training, and unlocked doors."

I sat up a little straighter in the chair. I'd wondered if he'd been too delirious, too out of it to remember promising me those things. He'd left my door unlocked this morning, but I could hardly believe that meant he'd finally put my sword in my hands.

"Your doors will no longer be locked, and you won't require a chaperone through the grounds." His dark eyes roamed across my body. "You're strong. You'll make a good warrior with a little training. That said, I think we both know you've had some before now. I saw the way you fought. An untrained fae would not have been able to do what you did with a simple metal sign."

I cleared my throat. Of course he would have noticed. Regardless of what innate abilities I might have, it took years of experience to train one's body to move as instinctively as mine did in a fight. Especially when I hadn't even had my sword.

"I've had some," I admitted. No use in trying to deny it. He might be cocky, cruel, and traitorous, but he wasn't daft. "I've met other solitary fae. One of them was a pretty good fighter, and he taught me some tricks."

"Hmm." His eyes flashed as he tapped his fingers against the arm of the chair. "You are still keeping secrets from me."

Surprise flittered through me. "And you're still keeping them from me."

He leaned forward, power rippling off his body in waves. "And what secrets would you have me spill, Moira?"

At the intensity of his gaze, my heart did a little flip. I wet my lips. "For starters, you could explain who those fae were who jumped us in the alley. They mentioned a cauldron. What's that all about?"

He regarded me carefully for a moment. "The Gundestrup Cauldron."

I shook my head. I'd never heard of it. "The gund-what?"

"Gundestrup." He let out a heavy sigh and shut his eyes. "It is an ancient magical vessel, made centuries ago. It comes straight from Faerie itself."

Wow. There weren't many things that still existed in this world that came from the fae realm. Most of those artefacts hadn't made it through the portal. The fae had fled to the mortal realm when ours had been destroyed. Not everyone had made it, and very few items had been brought along. Faerie had come back to life now, thanks to the Morrigan's reign, but most of the fae had stayed here instead of going back.

"Okay." My heart thundered in my ears. "What does it do?"

"Regeneration," he said, his voice pained. "It has the ability to bring someone back from the dead."

I wasn't sure what I'd expected him to say. Something along the lines of stealing a crown, growing an army, forging some kind of weapon that would never miss its mark. But bringing someone back from the dead? My mind churned. I didn't understand how that had anything to do with the throne or the Morrigan.

"So." I glanced at the books surrounding us, my eyes flashing from one title to the next. One on

Celtic items. Another on historical jewels. And yet another on the mythology surrounding metallurgy. These books were to help him find this cauldron. "Those fae in Barrie's Close. They're looking for this cauldron."

He nodded. "Some are members of this court."

I'd figured that much, especially with Warin poking around. "And...you're looking for it, too?"

"They're looking for it because they wish to bring someone back from the dead." His eyes went dark. "I'm searching for it to prevent them from doing it. Because of that, they want me out of the picture."

A strange fear flickered through me. "And who is it they want to bring back from the dead?"

He let out a long, shuddering exhale. "Nemain, the fae who tried to destroy the Morrigan. The fae who murdered dozens of innocents. The fae who would enslave the humans of this realm if she had the power to rule. They want her back."

13

I stared at Lugh for a long, long time without saying a word. My heart frantically ran laps through my chest, and my ears filled with a strange, electrifying static-y sound. Nemain had pretty much been the devil incarnate. She had killed my sister-in-soul, had murdered her in cold blood. Elise was dead because of her. And she wasn't the only fae Nemain had killed.

The Morrigan—Clark, the queen—had stopped her from destroying anyone else. And I had helped her do it.

When Nemain had died, I'd let out an exhale of relief so long that it was as if my entire world had been altered forever.

And now members of this court wanted to bring her back.

"You know her name," Lugh observed. "And you look like you've been punched in the gut."

I lifted my eyes toward his, my stomach churning. "Let me get this straight. Some fae want to bring Nemain back from the dead, and you want to stop them. That's why you're searching for the cauldron. Not to destroy Clark yourself. You don't want her crown?"

He levelled his gaze, steepling his fingers beneath his chin. "I may not want Clark Cavanaugh to be *my* queen, but I wish her no harm. As long as she doesn't bring an army to my gates, I will never make a move against her."

Oh. This conversation had certainly taken *a turn*. And I didn't know what to do with myself. I sprang out of the chair and started pacing through the room, but got frustrated when all the random books blocked my way.

I stopped suddenly, waving my arms around like windmills. "Why would someone want to bring back Nemain?"

He leaned back in his chair, an eerily-calm expression on his face. "I imagine because they would like to destroy the Morrigan and all the peace she stands for. Nemain promised a rule over every creature, where the fae were the dominant species. Humans would be nothing but bugs beneath our feet. The vampires and the shifters would be snuffed out completely. This world would be ours."

An angry rush of adrenaline pounded through me. I'd thought when we got rid of Nemain, we'd made it clear to every other tosser who thought that way that they were wrong.

"Who the hell is doing this?" I punched the air with my words. "I'll find them right now and put a stop to this. Is it Warin? I thought I saw him sneaking around the cliffs earlier, hunting for the hidden tunnel entrance. He's doing it. Isn't he?"

Lugh suddenly stood from his chair and loomed over me. "It isn't Warin. I asked him to check the cliffs and make sure he couldn't find it."

My mouth dropped open. "But...Saoirse said—"

Lugh shook his head. "It isn't him. She thought she had a reading that pointed to someone with red hair, but she said it was vague. Her prophecies are not always specific."

"Well, then we have to look at everyone else it could be. We have to—"

He rounded on me, suddenly standing only inches away. "*We?*"

At the strange intensity of his voice, I stopped my babble of incoherent thoughts. Taking a step back, I stared up at him. There was a hooded look in his eyes. A fierce electricity rippled across his skin. Not for the first time, magic sparked off his body, ricocheting against mine. I didn't know whether I wanted to run screaming from it, or if I wanted to step closer and let it consume me whole.

"How do you know so much about Nemain, Moira? Why are you so upset by this news? A solitary fae never would have had a confrontation with her. She was far too consumed by the Court."

His voice was steady and even, but it was dangerously soft.

Swallowing hard, I took a step back, but he closed the distance within an instant. I was quickly realising that I had misjudged him. Everything I'd thought was wrong. He wasn't working against Clark. He wasn't trying to steal the throne. And his cruel apathy was just a show, probably for the very same people he was working against.

We had somehow ended up on the same side...and I'd lied to him to get there.

I had to tell him the truth, even as hard as it would be. The second I spilled my secret, he'd toss me out of this castle. And he would likely never let me help him find the *real* enemy. But I couldn't keep going like this. He'd told me the truth. He'd opened up to me in a way I didn't deserve. And now I had to do the same.

I sucked in a deep breath and braced myself for his reaction. "I'm one of the fae who fought against her. I'm Moira Talmhach, a warrior fae in the Morrigan's Court. I'm not a solitary fae at all. I came here to...well, I came here to stop you from getting your hands on that cauldron and killing my queen."

The two words that whispered from his throat were the very last I expected to hear next. "I know."

"What?" I hissed the word and stumbled back. "What do you mean you know? You can't know. You let me in your Court. You've..."

I trailed off, and his wicked smile was my only answer. He knew?! All this time I thought I'd been playing him, but really he'd been playing me.

Letting out a roar, I shoved at his chest. The ridges of his abs beneath my fingers were unsurprisingly firm. He stayed rooted to the spot, that wicked smile still playing across his lips.

"Explain yourself," I demanded. "How did you know? Why the hell did you let me inside?"

"For one, I recognised you from that night at the Pack headquarters. I didn't know you were one of Clark's, but Saoirse did. She had a vision that saw you coming." He leaned forward, tucked his finger beneath my chin, and tipped back my head. I swallowed hard, my anger battling a strange churning in my core. "And I let you in because I have no fight against the Morrigan. If she wants to spy on me, then so be it...." His grin widened. "Plus, I thought it would be fun."

"Argh!" I slapped his hand away from my chin and whirled toward the door. That was it. I'd heard enough. He had purposefully tricked me into thinking I was some sort of hostage in this place. For what? Some fun?!

When I reached the door, I stopped to give him one last glare. "What about the blood contract?"

"I have it somewhere safe." He shrugged. "I can rip it in half at any time and the spell is broken."

"So you did all this to mess with me," I deadpanned.

"And you came here to spy on me. I'd say we're even."

"Oh no." I narrowed my eyes. "Just you wait."

And with that, I stormed out of the room, slamming the door behind me.

~

Despite my fury, I didn't leave the castle. I returned to my freezing cold room and huddled beneath a blanket by the window. At some point, an apologetic Saoirse stopped by with my sword and cell phone and said I was free to return to London whenever I wanted. The blood contract had been destroyed.

A part of me wanted to get the hell out, but my feet didn't want to cooperate. They refused to carry me down the steps and toward the train station. Instead, I made a call to Clark.

She answered half a ring into the call. "Moira?"

"It's me," I said with a sigh, gripping the phone tight in my hand. It was good to hear her familiar voice.

"Oh, thank god," she said in a rush of words. "I've been going out of my mind with worry. I got your note. The raven said you were fine, but...I was two seconds away from shifting into a bird and flying up there to rescue you myself. What the hell is going on? What do those numbers mean?"

I took a deep breath, half-afraid to spill the words and half-relieved I finally had the chance to confide in her. At least she hadn't translated the code and sent a band of warriors up here to storm the castle. Lugh had given me my truth and my freedom. He trusted that I wouldn't send an army straight to his front gates.

"Everything is okay. Kind of. It's a long story." I nibbled on my bottom lip. "I'm going to tell you something, and you're not going to like it. But I need you to make me a promise."

"Okay, now you're scaring me again," she said with a tense laugh. "What's the promise?"

"I need you to promise that you'll talk to Lugh before you make any decision about his claim."

"Claim?" she asked suspiciously. "What claim?"

And with that, I told her everything. Lugh, the Court of Wraiths, the traitors amongst them, and the quest for the cauldron that could bring back Nemain.

"He was never the one who wanted to go up against you," I finished. "He's been trying to stop them."

"I see." Her voice was hard. And tired. Very, very tired. I knew how she felt. The threat of

Nemain was back on the menu again only two short years after we'd ended it. Not to mention that Clark was expecting her first child now. She had far more to lose than she had before.

"What do you want me to do?" I asked her as I eyed my sword. The freedom was mine to take, if I wanted it.

"Do you trust him?" she asked.

I thought hard. Did I trust him? Yes and no. He'd made it clear that he wanted nothing to do with Clark's throne, but that didn't change the fact he'd made his own court out of fae who didn't want to be a part of hers. Some of whom were criminals. He could be cruel at times, but he could also be kind. And he was still hiding secrets. He may have opened up, but it hadn't been completely.

That said, I could hardly blame him for that. I'd been lying to him all this time myself.

I blew out a breath. "I believe he's sincere when he says he wants to stop the cauldron from getting into the wrong hands."

"Then I'd like you to stay there and help him, if you're up to it. I know how you must feel about the threat of Nemain...if it's too much for you, I can send someone else."

Elise's silver eyes flashed in my mind. My stomach turned. "No. It should be me. I'll stay."

~

An old familiar nightmare haunted my dreams that night. Cloaked figures scuttled after me in the dark, arms outstretched to reveal thin, bony hands. They whispered words of terror, filling my soul with a darkness so profound that I swore I would never see light again.

They wrapped their hands around me and pulled me to the leafy ground. Dozens swarmed me, pinning my arms against the dirt. They launched on top of me and squatted on my chest.

Images swarmed into my mind. Blood, guts, gore.

They poured their nightmares into my mind until they drove out everything else. All that existed within me was terror. And they fed on my fear.

I screamed, but no sound came out.

I was trapped inside the nightmare. Forever.

~

"You're still here," Saoirse observed at breakfast the next morning. I'd taken a long hot shower to rid my mind of my nightmares, scrubbing my skin until every trace of the darkness was gone. I'd dressed in my borrowed clothes and padded down to the Great Hall, hoping to find the only fae in this place who might understand me.

"You sound surprised." I plopped into the seat

next to her. The room was pretty empty. Most fae preferred to grab something to go from the kitchen for breakfast instead of dining in the formal Great Hall. I liked the arching timber beams myself. So did Saoirse, it seemed. "You didn't see what I was going to do with your..." I made a circular motion around my head, indicating her prophecies, her visions.

"I'm only half druid." She buttered a slice of toast. "So I don't have unlimited access to visions of the future. I have to choose my questions wisely. And sometimes, my visions are hard to translate."

"And so you asked a question when I got here," I said, nodding. Made sense. I would have, too.

"Nope. I've known you were coming for weeks. I found out when I did a read when...well, when I did a read about Tyr's death." She cast a glance my way. "The fae who had the room before you."

"Oh." So that was what had happened to the previous tenant. "How did he die?"

She nibbled on her toast. "Good question. That's what I was trying to find out, but the problem with my power is, it really only shows the future. All we know is that it had something to do with...the other stuff going on here. My vision seemed to suggest that you'd help. That's partly why Lugh wanted to see what you're made of."

I cast a glance around me at the fae in the hall. "Can you tell me what makes you think it's related, or...?"

"Tyr was on the warrior team. He was the one who found out about the..." She dropped her toast, glanced around, and then held her hands in the shape of a bowl. I nodded. The cauldron then.

A picture was now forming inside my mind. Tyr, one of the warriors, had been looking into things for Lugh. He'd found out about the cauldron, most likely gaining too much interest from the culprits. In the end, they'd killed him, which probably meant he'd gotten close to finding out enough to expose them.

So Lugh had taken a trip down south to seek out the services of a werewolf skilled in finding magical objects, in hopes of stopping the killers before they got their hands on the cauldron first.

And then I'd come along, crashing the party.

"I want to stay and help," I told Saoirse.

She swivelled on her seat, turning to face me, her purple eyes searching my face. "Lugh said you were very angry with him. I'd told him he was taking the whole thing too far, but he is Lugh, and he really didn't know what kind of honour you would have, if any."

"He was worried about my honour?" A new flicker of irritation went through me. "And does he really think it's honourable to commit treason against the crown? He's made his own secret court."

She sighed. "He never meant for it to be treason. He meant for it to be a hidden place for those of us who don't fit in anywhere else, who kind of want to hide from the outside world. Some of us have run from abusive situations. Some of us are former criminals, wanted by human authorities." And then she pointed at herself. "Some of us have powers that others would love to exploit."

My heart ached for her, but it pained me even more how wrong she was. About everything. "Clark is a half-shifter. She was on the run for years. If anyone understands how you feel, it's the queen."

"I'm sure she does." Saoirse dropped her eyes to the floor. "But she's too far away to protect us. She has her own concerns down south. You don't know what things were like here before Lugh came along and saved us. You don't know what Athaira—"

Her words ended in a choke, and ice went through my veins. Leaning forward, I whispered fiercely. "What are you talking about? What did Athaira do?"

Her purple eyes peered deep into my soul. "I can't talk about it."

Saoirse pushed up from the table, leaving her half-eaten toast behind. I jumped up and followed her toward the exit. "Where are you going?"

"We have a team meeting with Lugh at half past." She paused and gave me a solemn look. "You coming?"

Ten minutes later, I stood inside The Royal Palace. We were in one of the many empty rooms, the lofted ceiling arching overhead, dark blue walls surrounding us.

There were only a handful of us here. Lugh, of course, stood tall in the center of our circle. Saoirse and me, along with Warin and Boudica, clustered together. And, much to my irritation, the damn hobgoblin was here.

"It has become quite apparent," Lugh began with his hands tucked behind his back, "that the plot now involves more than just the return of Nemain. The fae behind this now wish me dead, too."

A chill swept down my spine at the matter-of-fact tone of his voice, like he hadn't just been stabbed repeatedly in the streets a few days ago.

"Filthy murderers," the hobgoblin spat. "I will wring their necks!"

I glanced at the tiny little creature, surprised. Hobgoblins were not known for displaying such intense loyalty, particularly toward fae. They liked to keep to themselves. Saoirse had been right. Lugh had opened the gates for the outcasts of the supernatural world, and they loved him for it.

Well, some of them. The others wanted him dead.

I raised my hand, and every eye in the room turned my way. "Yeah, hi. I'm a little late coming into this whole thing. Do we know anything about who they are? Anything that would help identify them?"

"They have sorcerer connections," Lugh said. "That's how they were able to collect the Sapphire."

"They're also growing in number," Saoirse added. "There were ten in the close, but only a few several months ago. That means they're meeting somewhere inside the castle without eyes or ears noticing, getting new recruits."

A deep frown dragged down the corners of Lugh's lips. "I reckon they're using part of the castle that rarely gets foot traffic."

"The old residential buildings, the ones that got destroyed during the witch trials," Warin said in a gruff voice.

We all turned toward the warrior who rarely spoke.

"They're on the western side of the castle, away from everything else. And it's nowhere near the front gates, so we don't watch it during our patrols. No one would really notice if fae were coming and going from there, at least not in the middle of the night."

Lugh gave Warin a grave nod. "That settles it then. Tonight, we will patrol the western buildings. We'll find the fae behind this attack. And we will deal with them."

Despite his morbid words, Lugh seemed to be in pretty good spirits when night fell. Maybe because he finally had something of a lead on the culprits. I had to admit the location made sense. If the traitors were going to recruit more Wraiths to their cause, the best place to meet in secret would be these buildings.

Our crew took to the cobblestone streets. Night had fully fallen, and thick clouds obscured the inky sky, smudging a full moon that hung low behind the city buildings. An icy wind knifed through the castle, and frost crunched beneath our boots. Even though we only planned to monitor the current situation, we'd all come prepared just in case we had to act. I had my sword back—the one Clark had gifted me. And Lugh had an imposing spear strapped to his back, silver tip jutting up toward the shadowy sky.

The old residential buildings were two imposing structures that formed a square, backing up against the western defences and the garden I'd cleared with Imogen. At one point in time, they would have been an impressive sight, but the windows were blacked out and soot crept up the stone sides. In the center of the courtyard sat another statue—or it had once upon a time. Now it was nothing more than a blackened husk in the shape of a man.

Our group split up. Saoirse happily went with the hobgoblin, for reasons I couldn't fathom, while the twins went together. That left me with Lugh as my only option, and I wasn't entirely sure how I felt about teaming up with him for the night.

Things between us were strained, and that was partially my fault. I'd stormed out on him, shouting and waving my arms. That said, I would only take part of the blame. He'd been playing me the moment I'd stepped through those gates.

We all split up to check the various wings of the

buildings, and I soon found myself alone with Lugh in the darkness. We didn't want to use any light, in case the traitors were nearby. They could come and go at any moment if they were using these buildings as their base of operation.

The halls still held the stench of smoke, even after all these years. As we cleared room after room, all I could think about were the fae who had once called this place home. How had they felt when their world burned down around them? Had they been captured by those in charge of the witch trials? Or had they retaliated?

Once we'd explored every room inside our designated wing, we found a room on the very top floor that gave a wide view of the courtyard below. The room was dark and empty, but it had barely been touched by the fire. We perched onto the floor beside the window and waited for the traitors to show.

Lugh was silent beside me, but I was all too aware of his presence. It was almost impossible to focus on anything else. Out of the corner of my eye, I could see the outline of his profile. The sharp, chiseled jaw, the glinting horns, and the hair that curled perfectly across his forehead. My fingers itched to reach out and brush it out of his eyes, but I bit my tongue instead.

After what felt like hours of tense silence, Lugh shifted from one knee to the other. "I didn't think you would stay."

"Yeah, well." I cleared my throat. "I had to help with the whole cauldron thing."

"Order from your queen?" he asked, doing little to hide the sneer in his voice.

I cut my eyes his way. "No, actually. Whatever you think about Clark probably isn't true. She gave me a choice. I decided to stay."

For a moment, he said nothing. Only silence hung between us, heavy and dark and suffocating.

"And it's just for the cauldron then," he finally continued, voice low. "Not for anything else?"

My heart skipped a beat. What was he even asking? Surely he couldn't wonder if I'd decided to stay because of *him*, right? Sure, there were rumours flying everywhere that we were in the middle of some kind of thing, and Saoirse couldn't stop looking at us with a knowing smirk on her face, but none of that meant anything.

We were practically enemies.

"Moira?" He twisted to face me, his brow furrowed. "You didn't answer my question."

"Oh." Heat flushed my cheeks. Luckily, we were in the shadows, and he couldn't see. "What other reason would I have for staying?"

"Right," he grunted and turned back toward the window.

With a frustrated sigh, I opened up my mouth to snap at him some more—it was becoming one of my favourite past-times—but a glowing blue orb rolled through the open door, distracting me from what I'd been about to say.

I frowned and pointed. "What's that?"

Lugh twisted to face it and cursed. "That's Sapphire. We need to leg it."

Without further ado, Lugh wrapped his arms around me and lifted me into the air. I let out a sharp cry, more alarmed by his bulging muscles than the blue smoke bomb about to obliterate our minds.

Clinging on tight, I peered down at the Sapphire as he hastened across the room. The glow brightened in a flash, and then a *pffffft* released the smoke. It surrounded us within an instant, dousing the entire room in a beautiful sapphire haze.

It only took about five seconds for the effects to hit me. One moment, I was annoyed, uneasy, and curious about the glowing orb. The next, I felt drowsy and kind of elated to be held in Lugh's arms.

They were such strong arms. I never wanted them to let go of me.

Lugh stopped rushing through the room, thank the Morrigan. All the motion was making me dizzy. I just wanted to stop and stare at the floating cloud. And his face.

He had a very nice face.

I wet my lips as he set me down, my feet finding the floor beneath us. Blinking up at him, I couldn't help but fixate my gaze on his chiseled jaw, those lips that pursed with irritation every time I went near him, and those eyes. They were as black as the darkest night.

Such nice eyes.

"Moira," he said in a low growl. "Stop looking at me like that. We've been hit by a heavy dose of Sapphire. Everything you're thinking, everything you're feeling, it isn't real."

A slight frown pulled down my lips. He was partly right. We had been hit by the Sapphire, and it was specifically meant to make someone pliable, enhancing their libido. It would explain why I wanted nothing more than to curl my body around his.

Nice face, nice eyes. And very nice body.

But he was also partly wrong. What I felt wasn't a lie, made up by some deep dark magic. I felt something for him, and it was very real.

A warning bell clanged in my head, and an ancient prophecy roared to life. One I couldn't forget. One that meant I could never, ever meet my mate.

I snorted and swayed on my feet. Silly little prophecy. Lugh wasn't my mate. He was the King of the Court of Wraiths. Whoever the unlucky bastard was who happened to be my mate, I hadn't met him yet. Hopefully, I wouldn't for years, if ever.

In the meantime, what was wrong with having a

little fun with this sexy-as-sin male? Practically purring, I rubbed my hands against his rock hard chest and leaned into him.

He shuddered in response, and he wrapped his arms around me. Tipping back my head, I peered up at him. Desire and danger swirled in his dark eyes, lighting magic up along my skin. His power curled through me, beckoning me closer.

"Do you want this?" he asked thickly.

"Mm hmm," I murmured, closing my eyes.

His lips crashed into mine as he kissed me with a fierce intensity that took my breath away. Gasping, I pushed up onto my toes and wound my arms around his neck. His hands slid down my back and skittered beneath my shirt, and he splayed his warm fingers against the small of my back.

Reaching up, I slid my fingers into his curly strands and clung on tight, pulling his mouth harder against mine. He groaned against me. The sound of his pleasure drove me wild. I didn't know what it was about him, but suddenly I couldn't get enough.

The kiss was great and all, but I wanted more.

I slipped my hands down his side, curled my fingers around his black cotton shirt, and then yanked it over his head.

Pulling back, he grinned down at me. He swayed a little, too. Or was that me? "Well, then. Someone sure does know what she wants."

"I've never been more sure about anything in

my life." I heard the words coming out of my mouth almost as though they were coming from someone else. It was as if a deep dark part of me had sprang to life, quashing down any and all caution. Logic had no place in my mind, not anymore. I wrapped my legs around Lugh's hips and pulled him down to the floor on top of me.

He growled and ran his hot mouth along my neck. Shivers raced through me, causing me to arch my back. My hands found his chest. I ran my fingers along the ridges of his washboard abs, his perfectly-sculpted pecs. His skin was smooth and hot and flickering with a magic that shot new waves of desire through my core.

I had not been lying when I'd said I was certain I wanted him. What was this Sapphire stuff? Some sort of truth potion? I knew it enhanced libido, but it was more than that. It was as if all my fears were suddenly gone. All that was left was the truth of what I really wanted deep down inside.

I slid my hands down his chest and fumbled with the button on his jeans. For a moment, Lugh froze, his breath puffing in front of me. And then slowly, almost excruciatingly, he reached down and wrapped his hands around my wrists. Wetting my lips, I flicked my gaze to watch his next movement. He pulled my arms over my head and pinned them to the ground.

Arching over me, he stared down into my eyes,

his own flashing with the same need churning through me. His pupils were heavily dilated; his cheeks were flushed with a deep crimson. He looked high. Hell, I probably did, too.

"What are you doing?" I whispered. "Kiss me."

And so he did. His lips pressed against mine, softer this time. His mouth speared mine, his tongue diving against my own. Moaning, I melted against him, wanting nothing more than to feel his lips on my body for as long as I could.

A little voice whispered in the back of my head, but I blocked it out. There was something I was forgetting. Something we were supposed to be doing. But whatever. I didn't care about that. All I cared about was Lugh.

My core ached from desire, and I arched my back to grind against his hips.

With a gasping breath, he pulled back and shook his head. For a moment, his eyes cleared, as if he'd shaken the Sapphire right out of his mind. "We need to stop."

"No," I murmured, reaching out for him. I, on the other hand, couldn't shake the Sapphire, and I didn't care one bit. Not when Lugh's body was pressed so tightly against mine.

He leaned down, growled, and nipped my ear. "I don't want it to be like this, drugged out of our minds. When I finally have you as mine, I want to be one-hundred percent in charge of what I'm doing. And I want you to know I mean it when I say I've never wanted anyone more."

He stood and grabbed his shirt from the floor. That was when we heard the scream.

14

The scream jolted me out of my Sapphire reverie. In a split second, I was on my feet and racing down the hallway behind Lugh. He tore out of the building and into the square, where the twins were circling the area, their swords raised high in the air.

"What happened?" Lugh barked. His spear was in his hands, even though I'd never seen him reach for it.

Warin spun on his feet, his eyes darting this way and that. "We heard a scream. Sounded like Saoirse. I don't know how they got by us."

Lugh swore. I knew what he was thinking. I was thinking it, too. If we hadn't been so distracted by our...ahem, activities, then we would have been on the lookout. We would have likely seen the attacker lurking around.

Distracted...

Frowning, I glanced up at Lugh. He met my eyes, his expression grim.

Of course. That Sapphire hadn't just appeared out of thin air, after all. It had been meant as a distraction, a way to keep us from peering out the window. We'd been tricked, and we'd fallen for it.

"You two search that way." Lugh jerked his head in the direction of the western defences and the cliff wall that plunged down toward the city. "Moira, you're with me. We need to find Saoirse. *Now.*"

Just as I started to jog across the courtyard, the hobgoblin stumbled out of the shadows, blood dripping down his side. He fell to his knees, yellow-green eyes wide as he gasped for air.

With a shout, Lugh launched toward him. He skidded to a stop by his side and scooped the little creature into his arms. The hobgoblin's ears flicked back, and his oversized feet flopped, as if the life had gone right out of him. My mouth went dry as I watched Lugh run out of the courtyard. Blood dripped onto the cobblestones with every step he took.

"Where are you going?" I jogged to keep up.

"I have to get him to the healers." Lugh tossed the words over his shoulder. "He can't heal like we can. Search for Saoirse."

Dread crept through me as I watched Lugh disappear around the side of the building, heading in the direction of the healing ward. I spun to glance behind me. The twins had already disappeared, searching their end of the courtyard for Saoirse.

It was just me out here. All alone to face the enemy. Judging from the wound in the hobgoblin's side, they were very much armed.

The Sapphire still churned through my bloodstream, chasing away most of the doubts and fears flaring in my mind. Gritting my teeth, I unsheathed my sword and stalked toward the spot the hobgoblin had appeared. The ground level of the building I approached was lined with several thick archways that led to the blackened underside.

With my back pressed up against the side of one of the archways, I peered into the depths, half-expecting a Sluagh to jump out and chomp me on the leg. In the distance, a clock chimed, startling me to the point I thought I might keel over from the intensity of my throbbing heart.

Why the hell was I so shaken up? I was Moira Talmhach, warrior and badass fae. I could do this thing.

It's just...it was really, really bloody dark beneath this building.

And so I did what every muppet in a horror film does. I inched into the darkness and called out, "Saoirse?"

Something slammed into the back of my head, and my sword was yanked out of my hands. Stumbling forward, I winced at the pain radiating through my skull. I whirled toward my attacker, fisted hands held at the ready, but I could see nothing more than the ripple of shadows in the night.

I'd been pushed deep beneath the building, and I couldn't see a damn thing.

A deep laugh echoed around me. "How does it feel getting hit by a metal sign?"

Ice slipped down my spine, and I jogged to the left, hoping I could confuse the attackers with where I'd gone. I had no idea how many of them there were. If it was the same as the attackers in Barrie's Close, it would be at least ten. Which meant I was sorely outnumbered. Without a sword, without backup, and without even a damn sign.

And they had all of those things.

"Not so tough now, eh?" another voice said, this one female. Was this the leader I'd seen fight Lugh? Maybe. Her voice sounded distantly familiar, like I'd heard it before.

I pressed my lips together, refusing to say a word. That would give away my location, and if I had any hope of getting out of this thing alive, I'd have to run.

An irritated sigh filled the silence. "Fine. We'll use our hearing then. We'll be able to find you just from your breathing."

Stilling my breath, I focused my own enhanced senses on my vision, letting the darkness fade into grey. I still couldn't see very well. Everything was a dusty, smudged painting, obscured by the extreme lack of light. But there were smudged forms shifting through the smog. It was enough to give me an idea of where they were.

And there, the looming shape of several ancient archways.

But while I'd been focusing on my sight, at least one of them had been sharpening their sense of sound. The second I moved, they would know exactly where I was. I had to act fast, but there was one last thing I had to do before I ran.

I took a very quiet sniff. Scents flooded my nose, battling each other for dominance. There was the stench of char that overpowered almost everything else, left behind from the fires that had plagued this castle during the witch trials. Beneath that, there was the unmistakable scent of lavender, along with oak moss, bloody iron, and crackling dead leaves.

"I think she's over there," a gruff voice said.

I darted toward the archways. My boots pounded hard on the cobblestones as I did little to mute my sound. There was no use, not when their enhanced senses were turned on. Even if I crept, they'd know where I was. Might as well charge.

A hand wrapped around my shirt as I skidded into the courtyard. It pulled me back toward the building, but I lurched away, throwing a kick at his head. He grunted and dropped my shirt, but several more attackers appeared behind me, blocking my way.

I glanced around, counting. Eleven this time.

Their number had grown, but not by many. Wetting my lips, I cast a quick glance toward the western defences. The twins weren't back yet.

"There's no one here to help you." The female fae stepped out in front of the rest, her face still obscured by the black cloth. "Give up, Moira."

My hands clenched. "Where's Saoirse? What have you done with her?"

"Saoirse is alive, which is more than I can say for you."

"Nice try with that Sapphire," I shot back, steering the conversation away from my impending death. "Where'd you get it?"

Maybe if I could get her talking, it would give me enough time for the twins to return to the court-yard. We'd still be outnumbered, but they had weapons. Together, we had a better chance of fighting these fae than I did alone. Mostly because these wankers had stolen my damn sword.

She chuckled. "Unlike you, I'm smart enough to know that nothing said in this castle can be kept a secret. You might not live to talk about it, but there's no telling who is lurking in the shadows listening in."

I mean, um, she had a point, but she was kind of missing an important part of the equation. If someone on my side was lurking in the bushes, they definitely wouldn't just squat there and watch me die!

At least, I hoped not. That would be a pretty jackass thing to do.

Wetting my lips, I took a step back, desperately trying to come up with another way to stall her. But I couldn't go far. The circle of traitors had now surrounded me, trapping me right in the center of the courtyard, next to the blackened statue.

I wasn't going anywhere. I had no weapon. They all had swords. I cut my eyes toward the statue. Nothing there I could use as a weapon. The best I could do was scrabble up and perch on the top, but they'd be able to yank me down easily enough.

I. Was. Screwed.

And every single one of them knew it.

The female leader drew closer, lifting her weapon. Heart hammering, I raised my fists before me. Even though I would never survive this thing, I wouldn't go down without a fight. I'd at least give her a broken nose for her efforts.

With a roar, she sprang toward me. I darted to the side, letting my training kick in. Even without my weapon, my magic slithered through my veins, moving my body at an impossible speed.

When she pulled back, I tried to dart to the right, but a traitor blocked my path. Narrowing my eyes, I glared at him. He didn't move. He didn't even blink. He just stood there like a stone guard, unmoving, unfeeling.

"What's this all about?" I jerked my thumb

toward her fellow traitor as she tightened her grip on the hilt of her sword. "There's one of me and eleven of you. Why not attack me all at once?"

She chuckled. "Do you want to get yourself killed?"

"No, I am honestly curious."

"You're Moira Talmhach, one of the best warriors alive. I want to take you down myself. One on one. A fair fight."

"Not really a fair fight when you won't let me have a sword," I mumbled.

But she didn't care. She swung her sword at my face. I ducked just in time to avoid losing my head, but the sword just kept following. It ripped through my shoulder, slicing deep into my skin. Pain lanced through my entire body as blood spurted into my face.

I fell to my knees, screaming. If the Sapphire had dulled pain and fear before, it didn't now. I couldn't even think around it. I could hardly even breathe.

Grabbing at my shoulder, my hand slipped against the thick blood coating my skin. I pulled my hand away and stared down at the red. There was so much of it. I was down on my knees. I was weaponless. All alone, surrounded by a dozen enemies.

I was going to die here tonight.

A deep-throated roar echoed through the court-yard, sending a new wave of panic through my gut.

The stench of blood and char filled the air as the darkness flashed with light.

Gritting my teeth, I pulled my gaze up from the cobblestones to see the traitors scurrying away from me, like ants away from rain. The female leader hesitated, flicked her gaze down at me, spat, and then ran.

The cobblestones rushed up to meet my eyes as I collapsed forward. Inwardly, I was desperate to see this new terror that had entered the castle, but my body refused to remain upright. My head was fuzzy, and a distant ringing had filled my ears.

Two strong arms wrapped around my body, and a dark pair of eyes peered into mine. Lugh. My heart constricted. He was here.

"Go after them," I let out in a hoarse whisper. "They have Saoirse. Don't let them get away."

His mouth set into a grim line, but he didn't move from my side. "You're hurt."

"But Saoirse—"

He cut me off by lifting me from the ground. The cobblestones fell away, causing a new wave of dizziness to rush through my head.

"You have to go after them," I said in a muffled voice as I realised that he was carrying me away from the square. The scent of char grew strong, and I caught sight of his five-pointed spear over his shoulder, smoking into the icy wind. "I'll be fine."

"You won't," he said firmly, jaw clenching.

"You've lost a lot of blood. She got you with the same weapon she wounded me with."

"Oh." My eyes slid shut. That made sense. No wonder I felt as though my life-force were flowing out of my body like a river. Because it was.

I cracked open my eyes to see the healing ward disappearing behind us. Frowning, I whispered, "Drop me off with the healers. You might still be able to catch the traitors."

"No. You're coming with me. They're busy with Uisnech. And besides, they don't have the antidote for this magic."

My mind tripped over his words. "Uisnech? Who the hell is Uisnech?"

"The hobgoblin." He cast his gaze down at me. "His name is Uisnech."

"Why do you have a hobgoblin named Uisnech in your Court of Wraiths?"

He gave me an incredulous look. "*That's* what you're worried about right now? Why I have a hobgoblin here?"

I tried to shrug, but it was kind of difficult with his arms wrapped so tightly around me. "He might be the most surprising part of this Court. Him and you."

"Me?" The pace of his footsteps quickened as the looming shape of the Royal Palace came into view.

"Yes, you. One minute, you're the most cruel fae

I've ever met, and the next you're cradling a *hobgoblin*."

"Uisnech is a strange, little creature, but I owe him my life."

Huh. That was not what I had expected him to say. There was a story there, one I was desperate to hear, but my head felt as heavy as lead. Tongue thick in my mouth, I asked, "How'd he save you?"

He cast a concerned look at my face as he reached the palace. With a quick kick, the door slammed open, and he rushed inside. Instead of heading into his quarters, he raced up the curving stairs and deposited me on a guest bed covered in very expensive looking silk sheets.

Silk sheets now stained with my blood.

Opening my mouth, I tried to snark about the price tag, but I was too tired. I flopped back onto the pillows and let my eyes slide shut.

I could still feel him moving around me, mostly because he kept shouting curses and stumbling into things. Why was he being so clumsy all of a sudden? He was Lugh, as smooth as steel and as unbothered as a lion stalking its prey. Something heavy pressed against my arm, and a magical warmth suddenly spread through my body.

The pain ebbed, though it didn't disappear. Instead of a piercing stab through my shoulder, it now felt like a dull, distant throb. Something else pressed heavily against the wound, and then, Lugh let out a long, shuddering sigh.

The pressure on my shoulder eased, and I felt, rather than saw, Lugh lean over me. "You're going to be okay. I got more antidote from the sorcerer after the attack in Barrie's Close, and it's stopped the bleeding. You'll feel weak for a day or two, but you'll be fine. You'll live, Moira."

His voice held much more raw emotion than I expected. My heart flipped over, and I was desperate to open my eyes. I wanted to look into his face. I wanted to reach out and touch him.

He wrapped his strong, warm hand around mine, and his forehead pressed lightly against my cheek. "I thought I'd lost you."

My throat was raw, but even if it wasn't, I wouldn't have known what to say. Did Lugh...have feelings for me? Terror swept through me at the thought. The prophecy. Caer's vision of my future.

The terror suddenly died.

The prophecy only mattered if Lugh was my mate, and he wasn't. We had no bond. There was no magic connecting the two of us together. When I closed my eyes, I didn't feel him there, deep inside of my soul. It was okay for me to reach out to him. It was fine for us to get involved.

Because if he wasn't my mate, I would not end up killing him.

My mouth went dry at the thought of the old prophecy that had haunted me all of my life. A druid had once told me she could see my future, one I could never avoid. I would one day meet my mate.

Our bond would be so strong that every fae who met us would know what we were.

And then I would murder him.

~

When I awoke, it was dark. I shot up straight in the bed, heart pounding like a runaway horse. Memories flashed through my mind. The traitors trapping me in the dark. The pain of the sword slashing into my shoulder. And then Lugh's terror-filled plea for me not to die.

I wasn't sure what scared me more.

Swinging my feet over the side of the bed, I stood and padded over to the window. I was still inside The Royal Palace, in the guest room where Lugh had tucked me for the night. The wound on my arm had begun to heal. The dull throb remained, covered by a thick bandage that I could poke without keeling over from pain.

I still wore my clothes from the fight, though Lugh had removed my thick leather jacket at some point. Along with my shoes and socks. Wiggling my toes, I pulled the elastic band from my wrist and piled my golden locks onto my head in a high bun.

I found my way down the stairs and knocked lightly on Lugh's open door. He sat on his sofa, surrounded by books. He was flipping through an old tome that wafted dust into the air, his tongue stuck out between his lips.

Lips that had been *all* over my body only hours ago.

He glanced up, and then snapped the book shut. In an instant, he was on his feet and crossing the room, concern painting his sharply cut features. "Moira? How are you feeling?"

I swallowed hard, awkwardness rushing through me. After our little make-out session and his strange emotional reaction to my wound, I didn't really know how to act around him anymore. We almost felt like strangers again, in a different dance than the one we'd been in before. That one had been easy. A snarky jab there, an angry outburst there.

Now, I felt...well, *shy* might be the right word, even though I'd never felt shy a day in my life.

"I'm okay," I said in a weird squeak. "Don't worry about me. You still might be able to catch them if you go now. At least search the castle grounds."

A strange expression flickered across his face. "No, I won't be able to catch them now. It has been two days, Moira."

My mouth dropped open. "*Two days?!*"

He gave a solemn nod.

"Two. Days?" I pushed at his chest. "You let me sleep for two bloody days?"

"You were drugged with Sapphire and healing from a fatal wound." He stepped back warily, clearly not expecting my angry reaction. "Your body needed time to heal."

I let out a frustrated grunt. "What about Saoirse?"

"Our team is looking into it." He took my hands in his, squeezing tight. "We've found a few leads. Hopefully, one of them will lead us straight to her."

My anger deflated a little. He'd been searching while I'd been out cold. At least that was something. "And, um, the hobgoblin...I mean, Uisnech. How is Uisnech?"

"He's fine." Lugh's lips twitched. "Though he's very worried about you."

"The hobgoblin is worried about me," I said flatly.

"It seems you've earned his very grudging respect," Lugh added. "First, you saved me in Barrie's Close. Then you took on a gang of traitors alone in order to help Saoirse. And when you earn Uisnech's respect..."

"Oh. Well." I swallowed hard and stared down at my bare feet. "Thanks for saving my life in return. I guess we're even now."

"It's not a game, Moira. We don't have points we can score. I'd do the same again for you in a heartbeat."

I lifted my eyes to his. "Even though I came here to spy on you for the Morrigan."

He nodded.

"Well, thank you." My cheeks flooded with heat. Clearing my throat, I said, "I'm feeling much better now, so I'll get out of your hair. I'll just grab my shoes and head back to my room."

"That is not happening," he said quietly.

"What? Why?"

He motioned for me to join him in his room. I picked through the piles of books and found a clear spot on the same armchair I'd chosen the last time I'd been here. Lugh settled back in on his sofa, placing the book he'd been reading on the table, a yellow bookmark poking out from the middle.

"I heard part of the conversation in the courtyard. The traitors want you dead."

Swallowing hard, I nodded. "Yep, sure seems that way."

"It seems their original target was Saoirse. At least, that was the plan for the night." He cleared his throat, eyes narrowing. "I have reasons to suspect they'll go after you again."

"It wouldn't surprise me," I agreed. "Though their main target is you."

"Perhaps." His eyes raked across me, sending a new swarm of goosebumps across my body. "They had a chance to attack us when we were...distracted. But they waited to go after you when you were alone."

My neck warmed. "Yeah, but you had your spear."

Why did that sound way dirtier than it was?

He leaned forward, bracing his arms on his knees. "They took Saoirse. They didn't try to harm her. I'd guess they plan to use her for her prophecy skills."

"But they tried to kill you in Barrie's Close," I argued. "Even if they wanted to use her for her prophecy skills, why the sudden change—oh."

He gave a slow nod, expression grim. "The only reason they wanted to kill me was because they were worried I'd get to the cauldron first."

"And if they're no longer trying to kill you, then they aren't worried about you finding the cauldron."

"Because they already have it."

My heart slammed against my ribs, knocking the breath from my lungs. "But...how?"

He held up a hand and slid his cell from his back pocket. Dialling a number, he put the phone on speaker and set it gently on the coffee table. After a few rings, the call picked up.

"Alpha speaking," Anderson's familiar voice crackled over the line.

"Anderson, this is Lugh. I was hoping you'd have some progress to report on for me. In regards to the cauldron. Eoin, one of my associates, mentioned you have a lead on its location."

A long moment passed before Anderson grunted. "I'm afraid it's a dead end. I won't be able to help you."

And then the line clicked off.

Slowly, I rose my eyes to meet Lugh's. "Anderson was pretty short there."

"He was indeed." Lugh steepled his hands

beneath his chin. "Seems someone else got to him and offered him a higher price."

"Bollocks." I jumped to my feet and paced to the large window overlooking the Crown Square. The fae sat atop the bronze horse, the statue as regal as ever. The exact opposite of my twisting insides.

"We shouldn't panic. There is some hope," he said quietly.

Lugh didn't know about my past with Nemain and why panic was the only option. I whirled to face him, my entire body trembling. "Nemain killed my friend." I shut my eyes. "No. *Friend* is too light of a word for what she was to me." I flipped them back open, spearing his gaze with mine. "My soulmate. My platonic soulmate."

Sadness filled his expression as he stood and crossed the room to wrap his arms around me. Shock flittered through me, but then relief. With a sigh, I leaned against him, giving in to the desire to take comfort in his touch. I breathed him in, fire, mist, and pine cones. Soothing scents, ones that massaged some of the ache in my heart away.

"If they've taken Saoirse, and they're targeting you, then they still don't have everything they need to bring Nemain back," Lugh said roughly, his mouth against the top of my head. "And I don't want them to get another chance at harming you. You'll stay here with me tonight."

15

I tried to argue my way out of The Royal Palace, but Lugh wasn't having it. After about five minutes of protestations, I finally gave up, partially because...well, I didn't *fully* want to leave. The room on the top floor of the residential halls was ice cold, and the temperature had plummeted over the past few days.

I didn't hate the idea of staying with him.

Together, we changed the sheets, tossing the blood-drenched set in the wash—probably in futility. The things were heavily stained. After helping me slide the final pillow into its sleeve, Lugh strode to the doorway and gave me a gruff goodnight.

Well then. I blew out a breath, shrugged out of my jeans, and settled back into the bed in only my tank top. The flannel sheets were cosy and comforting and drew me into sleep, even though I'd spent the past two days blissfully unaware of the world.

But then suddenly I snapped awake, my heart hammering. I didn't know if it had been two minutes or two hours, but something had very much startled me from sleep. I rolled out of bed and raised my fists before me...and then realised what had woken me.

A soft, lilting song drifted through the cracked door of the guest room. It had an aching, haunting sound to it, the kind of sound that wanted to burrow itself deep into my bones. I'd never heard anything quite like it, and a strange magic washed over me as I listened.

Was...was that Lugh?

Obviously, I had to find out.

Grabbing a blanket from the closet, I wrapped it around my shoulders and tiptoed into the hallway. The sound was coming from downstairs. From Lugh's quarters. I minced my way down the stairs and paused as I listened. Now that I was closer, I could tell it was a harp. I tiptoed the rest of the way to his door and peeked inside.

In the center of his living room sat a majestic, gold-trimmed harp that glowed in the darkness. Lugh sat before it, his eyes closed. His fingers whistled over the strings, that haunting melody rising majestically into the air.

I watched him, my jaw practically touching the floor. The King of Wraiths was just full of surprises.

First, he carried a hobgoblin to safety. Then he played an instrument like this with such soul, such emotion, that it brought tears to my eyes.

Nibbling on my bottom lip, my eyes caught on his biceps, his washboard abs, and his sculpted pecs. Yep, that's right. He wasn't wearing a shirt either, and I was flat-out gawking at him now.

That rumble went through my core again, and this time, it had nothing to do with the Sapphire.

But he had put me in the guest room, and not his own bed, for a reason. What had happened between us in the old burnt-out buildings meant nothing. I had been high, and he had been, too. Hell, he'd even stopped it from going any further than it had.

With one last longing glance in his direction, I back-pedalled to the stairs. I would leave him to it. And instead of bothering him now, I would go take a cold shower.

A very cold shower.

My back slammed into something fleshy. Hands wrapped tight around my arms. Heart leaping into my chest, I screamed and slammed my bare foot up behind me. It landed in my attacker's groin with a solid thunk, and a male voice groaned.

The arms released me.

I whirled, eyes flashing, fists raised before me. The attacker reached behind his back and pulled out twin glinting blades. I could only see his eyes.

They were a deep, deep blue. The colour of the darkest part of the ocean.

And then those eyes flicked up, widening as they stared over my shoulder.

I could feel him, even though I couldn't see him. Lugh strode out of his quarters, and an intense, lung-tightening power washed over me.

"You dare come into my quarters," the king rumbled, his voice as hard as steel, "and attack my guest beneath my roof."

The attacker's eyes gave me the impression that he was two seconds away from weeing in his pants.

I took that opportunity to jog back toward Lugh, my feet tripping over the blanket cape I still held tight around my body. Otherwise, the attacker was going to get an eyeful of my thong-covered bum.

A golden glint caught the corner of my eye, and I turned toward the King of Wraiths. He held his spear in his hands. The real spear. The one he kept locked up in a case. The five sharp peaks glowed as he pointed the weapon right at the attacker's gut, and the golden rivets whirled around the shaft.

Holy shit. What the hell was this thing? It was almost like it was...*alive*.

"Who are you?" Lugh advanced on the attacker. "What do you want with Moira? Who else is working with you?"

"I can't answer any of your questions," the attacker said in a fearful voice. "They'll kill me."

"*I'll* kill you," Lugh roared.

The enemy charged, his twin daggers slicing through the air. He aimed them right at Lugh's chest, and the pointed tips rippled with the threat of death. My body instinctively moved toward the danger, my arms outstretched to stop the daggers from sinking into Lugh's skin.

But Lugh's arm shot out, and he shoved me back behind him. He grabbed a shield from the wall with such speed that he looked like nothing more than a blur. The daggers slammed into the bronze, and then skittered off, like tiny pebbles against a brick wall.

The attacker's eyes widened as he stumbled back. Lugh advanced on him, growling. With one last frantic glance in my direction, the enemy pulled a gun from his pocket and pointed it right at me.

I froze, swallowing hard. It had been a long ass time since I'd seen one of those.

"I'll kill her," the attacker's voice wobbled. "She might have survived the sword, but she won't survive a gunshot."

Lugh made his move. In a terrifyingly split second, the world seemed to shudder against the pull of time. One moment, I swore Lugh stood tall with his shield held before him. I blinked, and then the five-pointed spear rammed deep into the enemy's chest.

Blood painted the floor.

Lugh jerked back his spear, and the body crumpled like a rag doll. I held a hand over my mouth as blood sprayed everywhere. On the floor, on the walls, on my bare feet.

Heart hammering, I glanced away. I'd seen a lot of death. I'd caused some myself. But this was a horrifying taste of brutality.

"Dammit, I didn't want to kill him," Lugh muttered, whirling on his feet and vanishing back into his quarters. I stared after him. Was that...was that it? Was he just going to return to his harp-playing now and pretend that there wasn't a dead body on his floor with blood spatter everywhere?

But he reappeared only seconds later, the spear whisked out of sight. My heart thudded as I watched him lean over the attacker's body. "What is that thing, Lugh?"

He glanced up at me, his eyes hard, but he didn't answer my question.

"Your spear," I pressed. "That's not a normal weapon. What is it? How did it move like that? Why do you keep it locked up all the time?"

He ground his teeth together, and turned his attention back on the attacker. "It is a very long story. One I'm not sure you're ready to hear. And right now..." He reached down and placed trembling fingers on the mask. "We need to see who this is."

He ripped the mask away. The face beneath it was not one I'd seen before, at least that I remembered. He had pale, freckled skin, pale hair that was almost white, and an upturned nose like a ski slope.

Lugh let out a heavy sigh, fisted hand braced on the floor.

"Is he one of the wraiths here?" I asked in a soft voice.

"No." He punched up from the floor and shoved his fingers into his hair, locks tangling around his horns. He'd gotten blood on his face, but I decided not to point that out just yet. "He was part of Athaira's lot. One of the few who liked her reign and was angry when I took over here. He left the castle months ago. I didn't expect he'd come back, but I guess I was wrong."

"Ohhh." That made a lot of sense, based on what Saoirse had told me. I still didn't know the full story, but I did know that Athaira had been cruel. If the fae who had actually liked Athaira still held a grudge... "So does this mean we were wrong? That these traitors aren't traitors at all, but more like...usurpers."

"I'm the usurper," he said roughly. "I took the castle from her after I learned of the abuse she rained down on her weaker subjects. These fae want their castle back. And they want Nemain to rule it instead of me."

"But that's kind of good news, right? It means that none of the wraiths here are working against us. It's people who left."

He shook his head. "There will be at least one. Someone is letting them inside the castle, and is feeding them information. For example, they knew you were staying here at the palace, and they knew that I would be playing my harp, which would drown out the sounds of an attack. If I hadn't been paying attention…"

I cocked my head at him. "How would anyone have known you'd be playing the harp?"

"I play it every night at eleven." He gave me a long, scorching look from head to toe. "You're covered in blood. You should take a shower."

I pointed at my face. "You have some blood on your cheek."

His eyes softened, and he strode across the floor. "There's some in your hair as well. Come along. Let's get you clean."

My heart thumped, though the flicker of excitement was quickly doused as I tiptoed across the floor. "What about this...mess?"

"Uisnech will take care of it. He will find good use of the blood."

My footsteps faltered, but his hand quickly found my back, propelling me along. "Do I want to know what a hobgoblin does with blood?"

He let out a low chuckle. "He sells it to vampires. Fae blood is highly potent. And extremely valuable."

Stomach twisting, I frowned. "Is it really a good idea to sell fae blood to vamps? What if they get a hunger for it?"

"They already have a hunger for it, Moira," he said smoothly. "Selling it to them prevents them from trying to take it by force. And none of us here wants a supernatural war in Edinburgh."

Lugh led me to a door at the end of the hallway, opposite from the room that led to his quarters. Inside, an expansive bathroom gleamed before me. A large claw-footed bathtub sat before a floor-to-ceiling row of windows that overlooked the cliffs. To the right, there was a long stretch of sinks, the counters crafted from a charcoal marble. On the opposite side was a shower. The kind with the rainforest shower-head and jets that shot out from the side. The door to the shower was see-through glass, and the cubicle itself could fit at least two people, maybe more.

"Let me take that blanket," he murmured, and I realised I still clutched the soft material tightly around my body. Nervously, I handed it to him.

His eyes darkened. "Don't look so afraid. I won't bite you."

That's a shame.

Lugh leaned past me and flicked on the shower. Hot water poured from the large shower-head. Before I understood what was happening, he'd lifted my shirt over my head. Which meant I was now wearing nothing more than my bra and panties.

His eyes scorched across my body. "Go on. Ladies first."

Heart thudding against my ribs, I stepped under the soothing spray of the water. Lugh began to turn away, seemingly to give me some privacy, but I cleared my throat. He paused.

"You need to shower, too," I said quietly.

His lips twitched, and in an instant, his clothes were a puddle of cloth at his feet. I kept my gaze rooted to the spot, which was the tiny little knob about chest height. I didn't let myself look at him, mostly because I was scared I might turn into a puddle myself.

Was he wearing pants?

My eyes flicked down. Damn them. The traitors. No, he was not wearing pants.

He was very, very naked.

I couldn't take it any longer. Twisting around to face him, I wrapped my arms around his neck and crushed my lips against his. For a moment, I was scared this shower idea of his had been nothing more than a way to get clean, but then a groan seeped from his parted lips.

His hands slipped down my back, splaying across the curves of my bum. With a sharp tug, he pulled me closer, his kiss deepening.

"*Excuse me!*" a shrill voice echoed through the marbled bathroom. "You have a dead fae lying in your entryway!"

Lugh growled, twisted away, and cracked the door just enough to stick his head around it. Steam billowed around us, obscuring the view, but I'd recognise that voice anywhere. "Uisnech. I told you to wait. I am otherwise occupied. I will be with you in...an hour."

An hour?!

"Yes, you see, but the door to the palace was wide open, and you see...there's a crowd. And they are extremely frightened, my dear king."

Lugh swore. He released me and vanished from the steamy shower. Through the fogged glass, I could see the outline of his shape. One moment, he was the male I'd wrapped my arms around. The next, he was taller, more commanding, just *more*. He was the King of Wraiths.

16

It had been three days since Saoirse had been taken, and the entire Court was on edge. Uisnech had cleaned up the mess, but half a dozen fae had seen the gore first. News had spread like wildfire, and everyone was too afraid to step outside their rooms at night.

Truth be told, I didn't blame them.

For the past two nights, I'd stayed in the Royal Palace guest room, but Lugh had been gone for most of it. At night, he would disappear after playing his harp for an hour, doing who knew what. I never asked him. I assumed it had something to do with Saoirse's disappearance.

Tonight, however, things were different. He'd called me into his room just before ten. Uisnech stood in the corner, rubbing his hand against his chin.

"What's going on?" I glanced between them. "Have you heard something about Saoirse?"

"The enemy has called. Saoirse can go free. For a ransom." Lugh's words were clipped, his expression betraying nothing.

"Are you serious?" I strode further into the room, my heart tripping. "What did they say?"

"They want to exchange you for Saoirse," the little creature piped up. His expression was nowhere near blank, like Lugh's, though he was just as hard to read. Nose twitching, his eyes swirled with a mixture of delight, curiosity, but also somber dread.

"Trade for *me*?" I gazed from Lugh's blank face to Uisnech's strangely somber one. "Why the hell would they want to do that? I have nothing that would help them."

Lugh pursed his lips. "Unfortunately, they disagree."

My heart thumped hard, and I hated that I couldn't read his damn face. I knew he cared about Saoirse. They had a bond I didn't understand. Would he willingly toss me to the enemy in order to save her life? And could I even blame him? I wanted to save her, too. "It doesn't make any sense. What was your answer?"

At that, he finally shifted his eyes to meet mine. "I told them no."

I actually didn't know how I felt about that. Somewhat relieved, if I were being totally honest. That meant he cared about me, too, and that sent a buzz of electricity through me that I hadn't expected.

But then a jolt of frustration joined the much more pleasant emotions. Saoirse was a smart, savvy, intelligent fae. Well, druid fae. But she wasn't a fighter. She wasn't skilled in combat. I respected the hell out of who she was and what she could do, but if it came down to a physical fight, she'd lose. I'd seen those traitors in the streets. They'd been trained.

I levelled my eyes at Lugh. "We have to take them up on this offer. It's been days since her disappearance, and we've learned nothing about where they might be keeping her. No leads. Not even a lead for a lead. This might be the only chance we have to save her."

"I told you that's what she'd say," the hobgoblin hissed toward Lugh.

"Uisnech thinks you're some kind of noble warrior," Lugh said dryly, "but what he doesn't understand is that surrendering you to Athaira's lot will be signing off on your death sentence."

I crossed my arms. "Really? After everything we've been through, you still don't have confidence in my ability to take on these cauldron tossers? I can take care of myself, Lugh."

"They won't accept the trade if you carry a sword with you," he replied. "And I doubt they'd let you anywhere near something you could transform into a weapon, like that sign."

"I don't need a sword," I shot back. "I only need a blade. Or a few dozen. Yeah. I like the idea of a dozen."

Uisnech smiled wide, his yellow-green eyes crinkling in the corners. "Clever as well as brave!"

Honestly, it was nice the little guy didn't want to feed me to the Sluagh anymore, but this newfound devotion was a bit much.

"Explain," Lugh said in a low growl.

"My skill is with the blade. Knives work, just not as effectively. I like the feel of a sword, and I love how the steel sings when I swing it. But I can be deadly with something smaller than that."

Lugh twisted toward Uisnech, who gave an eager nod. But then he scowled. "No. Absolutely not. I'm not sending you to those fae."

"It's not up to you," I said with a shrug. "I'm not actually part of your Court, remember? I can do as I please." Then, I turned to the hobgoblin, whose little green ears were twitching with excitement. "Uisnech, do you think you can hook me up with a few knives and figure out how to hide them in my clothes?"

The hobgoblin nodded eagerly. "Oh, yes, my love."

For once, I didn't hate the moniker. I grinned at Uisnech and gave him a high five.

Lugh scowled, of course.

～

*T*he Cauldron Tossers—my favourite new nickname for them—wanted to do the trade in Gilmerton Cove, which was a half hour drive south from the castle. Much like the vaults where I'd been forced to fight the Sluagh, Gilmerton Cove was a tangle of underground chambers and tunnels. No one knew quite what the tunnels had once been used for. It was one of Edinburgh's favourite mysteries. Many theories abounded. A smuggler's lair, a secret drinking den—for humans or vampires, no one knew—or even a meeting place for the Knight's Templar, who had been fae.

I leaned more toward the obvious choice—that it had once been a haven for sorcerers trying to escape the witch trials. They'd holed up underground, waiting for the burning torches to pass them by.

Lugh had grudgingly agreed to go through with this plan. On one condition. I wouldn't actually turn myself over to the Cauldron Tossers. Instead, we set a little trap.

The trap was this: I would descend into the tunnels while Lugh and the ginger twins stood watch and trailed my every move from the shadows. As soon as the Cauldron Tossers showed themselves, we'd all fly into fight mode, including me. Uisnech had succeeded in hiding ten different daggers on my body. We'd tried twelve, but the extra two just wouldn't fit.

Standing alone outside of Gilmerton Cove, I eyed the small mining cottage warily. It looked pretty normal, as far as secret hideouts for murderous supernaturals went. The little white house sat on a nondescript road cutting through a southeastern suburb about four miles outside of Edinburgh's city centre, squatting right next to a vet clinic.

I tapped the hidden bluetooth mic and whispered, "You lot sure this is the right place?"

"Affirmative," Uisnech replied in a giggle. This whole mic thing had been his idea. Something he'd seen off of one of those American SUV or CSI shows, or whatever they were called. Everyone was listening in. The twin warriors, who were nearby and watching my every move. Lugh, who lurked in the pub across the street. And Uisnech, who had stayed behind at the castle to oversee the guard team there. Even though we were out prowling for the Cauldron Tossers, the castle still needed protection, just like always.

I rolled my eyes and pushed open the door, surprised to find it completely unlocked. Inside, I found a flight of stairs with only about a dozen steps leading into shadowy darkness. There was a bright red arrow taped to the wall, pointing downward. Gee, which way should I go?

"Current status," the hobgoblin's voice rang in my ear. "Echo, stat, affirmative."

I huffed. As much as I was starting to like the

creature, I wished he would stop buzzing nonsense into my ear. "I'm inside. There's a flight of stairs. I'm heading down it."

"Careful, Moira," Lugh warned.

I gave a nod, even though he couldn't see me, and a slight ripple of panic went through my gut. My feet hit the first stair, and memories flooded my mind. Sluagh lurching out of the shadows. Creatures pinning me to the ground. I shook the thoughts away and continued downward.

When my feet hit the bottom stairs, I flicked on my torch. A long dark tunnel stretched before me. Wetting my lips, I pressed onward, hoping that the twins were right behind me.

"What do you see?" Lugh's voice crackled in my ear.

I whispered into the mic. "Dark tunnel. No one's here."

The crackle erupted in my ear, and I grimaced, smacking my hand against my head. A second later, the static vanished. I poked at the mic. "Hello?"

No response. I poked it again and whispered Lugh's name. Again, no response.

Great. Now I had no contact with the outside world. Down in the underground chambers, the signal was blocked. Still, I continued forward, heart hammering. Saoirse's life was hanging in the balance, and I wouldn't turn my back on her.

Somewhere ahead of me or behind, I heard the unmistakable echo of footsteps. My heartbeat sped up, and I flicked my torch left and right. The tunnel twisted left, and I followed, feeling like prey walking straight into a trap. At any moment, the big bad wolf would lurch out of the darkness and chomp me in half.

A hand pressed against my back, and I screamed. I whirled in an instant, dagger in my hand. Warin blinked back at me, his hands raised before him. "Whoa. Moira. Chill. It's just me."

Swallowing hard, I jogged a step back, my daggered hand still raised before me. "What are you doing sneaking up on me in the tunnel like this? You're supposed to stay hidden."

And he'd just totally given us away. If the tossers were watching, they'd know I'd come with backup.

"You've been walking in a circle. Boudica and I searched every chamber, and I've been using my enhanced hearing this whole time. No one is here. The whole place is empty."

My stomach dropped to the floor. "What? But this is where they told me to come."

He shook his head. "I know they did, but they must have left."

"Is there another way out of here?" I asked.

"Not that we could see."

"But you would have heard if someone else had been in here and left?" I prodded.

He pressed his lips into a grim line. "Yep. I had my hearing tuned in the entire time, and the only other fae I heard down here besides Boudica and me was you."

"Bollocks." I pushed past Warin and rushed back down the tunnel, and then charged up the stairs. All the way, I poked at the mic, waiting for the crackling static to return.

When I reached the top of the stairs, Uisnech's cheery voice rang in my ears. "Echo, beepedo ten four!"

"Uisnech. No one's here. It must be some kind of trick to get us out of the castle." My heart hammered. "I think they're heading straight for you."

17

The castle was in chaos when we returned. Fae were streaming across the courtyard, some charging into the Great Hall and others pounding on the front doors of The Royal Palace. On the way back, Uisnech had kept us updated through the bluetooth mic system until he'd abruptly cut off. Now he met us as we returned through the hidden back tunnel.

He leapt toward us as we climbed out of the car. "About twenty of them showed up. They came in this way, and we didn't see them because the guards were watching the front gates. They swarmed the Royal Palace after setting off a bunch of fires to distract us from what they were really doing."

"The palace?" Lugh's voice went sharp. "Did they...?"

The hobgoblin shook his head. "I had enough warning to hide the spear."

I cut a sharp glance Lugh's way. The damn spear again. Why would Uisnech need to hide it from the attackers? I wanted to ask, but I knew Lugh wouldn't tell me now, not with everything else going on.

"They trashed the palace looking for it," Uisnech continued, "but when they realised it wasn't there, they ran."

Lugh stopped short. "They just left?"

Uisnech gave an eager nod. "They came here for the spear, but they weren't prepared to fight. When I finally got the guards charging toward them, they fled. I managed to get a few photos of some of them when their masks got ripped off during the fight. I'll send you the images. None of them are members of the Court, not that I saw."

Lugh swore and dropped back his head to stare up at the sky. "I don't know what this means. How did they know about the back gate? Have they determined how to use the cauldron? Is that why they're after my spear? Or are they just getting desperate?"

"Hi. Lugh." I tapped his arm. "I might be able to help more if I knew the deal about your spear."

"Not now," he growled. "But we clearly need to keep it hidden from now on." He turned toward the twins, who were watching the entire exchange with flashing eyes. "You two, help the rest of the team round up the fae. I'll give a speech in the Great Hall shortly, as soon as we ensure the gates are secure.

We'll have to shut down this entrance since the enemies know where it is now."

The twins gave a nod and set off across the courtyard toward the scrambling fae.

Uisnech blinked up at Lugh. "What would you like for me to do, my king?"

Lugh grasped the hobgoblin's shoulder and gave it a squeeze. "You've done enough tonight, Uisnech. Recharge. Go have your feast."

I cocked my head, new questions swirling through me. What the hell was the hobgoblin's feast? And did I really want to know? Uisnech gave Lugh a brilliant smile and disappeared down the tunnel, heading toward town instead of the castle.

Lugh strode in the direction of the Great Hall, and I fell into step beside him. "What are you going to do now?"

"Now." He raked his hand through his midnight blue hair. "I have to be the King of Wraiths."

~

After Lugh gave a speech to his wide-eyed and fearful fae, they seemed to calm down, at least a little. He'd called the entire Court into the Great Hall where he'd sat on his throne of twisting vines, fielding questions. His voice had been calm and soothing, but he'd also stood his ground in such a way that they couldn't help but listen to him. He had ordered them to return to their rooms and get some rest. There were enemies out there, he told them, but he would keep them safe.

He had said he would be the king, and he'd been right. They needed him, and he'd lived up to their expectations. It was a damn important trait for a king, and I couldn't help but feel a bit of respect for him myself.

Afterwards, he asked me to join him back in the palace. The traitors had completely trashed his quarters, desperately searching for his magical spear. I helped him clear it up a bit, stacking torn books against the wall and sweeping up broken glass. In the end, his room ended up as close to clean as it normally was, which wasn't saying a great deal.

He sank into the sofa and dropped his head into his hands. "Everything is spinning out of control, and I don't know what to do about it. Tonight I put these fae's lives in danger. That's not even counting the fact that Saoirse is still in trouble. I hate that she's out there and there's nothing I can do. If anything happens to her, I'll never forgive myself."

I pressed my lips together. "We'll find her. We just need to think two steps ahead of the enemy instead of two steps behind."

Not that I had any idea how to do that.

"I should do something." He pushed up and stalked to the broken window, glaring out at the dark night. It was almost midnight. There was nothing we could do. "I should go out there and rip the city apart until we find her."

"Lugh. I'm not sure using your brute strength is the right course of action right now, not in a city full of innocent humans."

Softly, I stepped toward him and joined him at the window. The cool breeze fluttered my hair away from my shoulders, making me shiver. With a glance down, he wrapped an arm around me, rubbing his warm hands along my chilled skin.

I tried to keep my face blank. It was impossible. My whole body had lit up from his touch. Even after everything that had happened, all the danger and the terror, I still wanted him more than ever.

"There must be something we can do," he insisted. "Something they don't expect."

An idea sparked in my mind. "Actually, I do have an idea. Uisnech got some photos, right? I'll send them to Kyle, who is this master hacker friend of mine, and he might be able to get a trace on them. I bet they won't see that one coming."

Lugh didn't look particularly thrilled by my brilliant idea, but he didn't argue as I made the call. Even at this late hour, Kyle answered. I quickly filled him in on what had happened and shot the photos over to him. He promised he'd at least find something for us within the day. Thanks to CCTV, he'd be able to get a hit on their faces by hacking into the human databases.

I hung up the phone and gave Lugh a weak smile. "Kyle's on the case. He's going to use his famous hacking skills to track down their registered addresses. Now we just have to wait."

"I don't like asking for help from the queen," he muttered.

"Well, that's fine then," I replied. "Because *you're* not asking for her help. All I did was call up an old friend of mine."

"It's more than that, and you know it. He's a member of her Court."

I propped my fisted hands on my hips. "Is that what you're upset about? If that's how you feel about help from members of Clark's Court, then you should have sent me away in the first place. *I* am a member of her Court, too, you know. Why the hell keep me around if the queen's help bothers you so much?"

"Because," he growled, but I never heard the end of his sentence. He twisted toward me and sank his lips onto mine. With a gasp, I leaned into the kiss, wrapping my hands through his tangled hair.

His hands slipped down around my bum, and he lifted me from the floor. I wrapped my legs around his hips and arched against him. He growled, and his hard length dug into my thigh.

His kiss deepening, he began to stride across the room with his arms wrapped tight around me. He carried me into the bedroom and kicked the door shut. Heart pounding, I pulled back and stared into his inky eyes.

"I thought you didn't want to do this," I

whispered.

"I didn't want to do it when Sapphire was rushing through our veins," he murmured, teeth nicking my neck. "But I very much want to do it now, knowing that your want for me is real and not manufactured by drugs."

Oh, it was real. It was very, very real.

Lugh set me gently on the bed. He stood back and surveyed me, his fingers dipping to the buttons on his jeans. Swallowing hard, I watched as he stripped to nothing. His clothes formed a pile around his feet until nothing but his full masculine glory was before me. Heat flooded through my body as I gaped. His entire body was corded with pure muscle that rippled as he moved.

"Your turn," he murmured.

I stood and pulled my shirt over my head without hesitation. As he watched me with fiery eyes, I pushed down my trousers and toed out of my panties. Even though he'd done nothing to touch me since the moment we'd begun undressing, my core was aching and my nipples had hardened.

I didn't even know how I was breathing. *Was* I breathing?

Lugh grabbed my hips and lifted me onto the bed where he tipped me back onto the blankets. Spreading my thighs wide, he leaned over me. His length pressed against me, teasing me, making shockwaves of desire shoot through my core, but all he did was smile.

I reached up and dug my fingers into his thick strands, pulling his mouth down to mine. He groaned against me, tongue twisting with mine. His fingers trailed up my sides, and his hands cupped my breasts.

My thighs tightened around his hips instinctively.

But he took his time. His tongue lapped against my peaked breasts, teasing and sucking and taunting me with each exquisite stroke. Wriggling under his touch, I dropped back my head and moaned so loud that my voice echoed off the ancient lofted ceiling.

Lugh didn't seem to care. Instead, it seemed to excite him even more.

He pulled back, sucking in a breath as his midnight eyes raked across me.

"You're the most beautiful woman I've ever seen," he said in a deep growl.

Smiling, he dropped back down to kiss my stomach, his lips trailing across my skin, his fingers digging into my hips. My whole body shivered with anticipation as his mouth went lower—and lower. Until it hovered teasingly just an inch from my core. He leaned forward and dragged his tongue between my aching thighs.

And *oh my god*, I'd never felt anything like this before in my life. I couldn't stop my body from bucking on the bed and my legs from tightening around his neck.

"Oh, you like that, do you?" he murmured

before diving back in. His tongue slid inside of me, sending new shockwaves of pleasure through my trembling body.

I wanted more, more, more, but it felt so bloody good that I couldn't hold on anymore. His fingers dug into my hips, and that was it. My orgasm stormed through me so hard and so fast that my ears roared with the thunder of my exhilarating release. My body shook and shuddered, my thighs squeezing tighter around him.

"That was just the beginning." Lugh shot me a wicked smile as he stood and lifted me from the bed. I kept myself wrapped around him, heart hammering hard enough to shake the very ground on which we stood. He carried me across the room and slammed me against the wall. Books fell all around us, joining the mess.

His need was hungry now and fierce. He growled as he nipped my neck, his length pulsing hard against me.

And then his grip softened. Loosened. His mouth opened, and his tongue pressed through my lips. Moaning, he began to kiss me hard, sending shivers of delicious magic through my veins.

I sighed against his lips, relishing in the feel of him. The hard planes of his stomach shifted against my body where he trapped me against the wall.

"I want you, Moira," he breathed as he pulled back to meet my eyes. The coldness I first saw in him was completely gone, replaced not only with heat but with warmth. Something was happening between us now, something far more than sex. And it made my pulse race even more than it had before.

Because I felt it. Deep in my gut. I wanted the King of Wraiths more than I'd ever wanted anything before.

My entire body trembled.

Gently, Lugh slid his cock inside of me. It hurt, just a little, but I found pleasure in the pain, dropping my head against the wall to moan loud enough for the rest of the Court to hear.

Luckily, the walls were soundproof.

His mouth massaged my ear, my throat, my lips as his length thrust in and out of me. I held on tight, my fingernails digging deeper into his skin with each and every slam against the wall. I could feel my core clenching tighter, the desire and lust building up inside me to an overwhelming crescendo.

It was all I could feel. It was all I could see. Nothing else existed in this world but us.

His pace became rougher, quicker.

"Lugh," I panted, squeezing my thighs tighter around his hips. "Lugh, I—"

I cried out, clutching his shoulders like a lifeline as the orgasm ripped through me, harder and faster than I'd ever felt before. He shoved into me one last time, grunting out my name as his cock hardened and then throbbed hard, his seed pouring inside me.

We panted, clinging onto one another. My ears rang, and my throat felt hoarse from my screams. I had no idea how or why this had happened, but I never wanted it to end.

~

Blood singing with magic, I traced lines on Lugh's chest. He twisted to face me, sleepy satisfaction shining in his eyes. He rubbed his hand against mine, pressing my fingers tight against his beating heart.

"I enjoyed that," I said with a smile. "Very much."

"I bloody hope so," he said with a chuckle. "Otherwise, your screams meant something very different."

"Hmm." I kissed his chest. "You're very good at that."

"So it seems." He sounded very pleased with himself. "I am happy to oblige your needs any time you'd like."

A thrill went through me. "What about...now?"

We'd only just finished ten minutes ago, but I was already feeling that need again. All he had to do was look in my direction and I wanted him. And we were doing far more than that now. I was naked. He was naked. Our bodies were pressed together. There was no telling how much longer I had here at the castle. Might as well make the most of it.

"I hate to break up this moment," he murmured. "But I need to check on my spear before another round. Uisnech hid it for me, but I need to see it for myself."

That thing again? I pushed up onto my elbow and stared down at him. "Are you finally going to tell me what the deal is with that spear?"

He sighed and closed his eyes, his long lashes splaying across his cheeks. "I want to tell you everything, but I must admit, I fear what you will think of me."

Every now and then, I could tell that Lugh had been alive for a very long time. His modern speech would slip, and the formality would roll back in.

I rolled over on top of him and slid my fingers into his hair. "There's nothing you could say that would change my mind about you."

He opened his eyes, pulled my face toward his, and kissed me deeply. "This is hard for me. I've only ever trusted two people in this world with my secret."

A flicker of hurt went through me. "Does that mean you don't trust me enough with it?"

"No, Moira." He sighed. "It means I do. I'm just afraid I'm wrong, and you'll run away from me."

What could he say that would make me run? After what we'd been through together, after everything I'd seen him do. He was a good male. A great one, really. So what if he had a crazy powerful spear?

Lugh grabbed my hips and slid me off his body,

and then swung his legs over the side of the bed. He grabbed his pants from the floor and tossed me an oversized t-shirt of his. "Come on. We'll check on the spear, and I'll show you what it is."

My heart beat rapidly, and I pulled the shirt over my head in record time. He was finally going to tell me about his spear. I'd known there was more to the weapon than met the eye, and I eagerly wanted to know the full truth of it.

I padded after him. He led me to the end of the hallway, where I noticed he'd begun to pile some books on a shelf. My lips quirked. I'd been the one to suggest a bookshelf. And I felt kinda smug that he'd listened.

Lugh reached beneath the top shelf, and a click echoed through the quiet palace halls. When the shelves swung inward to reveal a hidden passageway, my mouth fell open.

"Huh. Okay, that's pretty wicked." I squinted as I peered inside. A long tunnel stretched out before us, swinging to the right. "Where does it lead?"

"To a room that no one knows about but me, Uisnech, and now you," he said quietly. He reached inside and flicked a light switch, the hidden tunnel suddenly illuminated by a soft glow. "Come. I'll show you the spear."

Eagerly, I followed behind him. We padded down the hallway, and then made the turn right into a small room about the size of the one where I'd stayed in the residential building. There was a small cot lining one wall, and a desk on the other, hidden beneath mounds of books and papers. A space heater was plugged into the wall socket. Sitting right beside said wall socket was the case-enclosed spear.

Even though I had seen it several times by now, it still took my breath away. The magic seeped into the room, filling it up with a buzz of electricity that smudged the thoughts in my head.

Instinctively, I moved toward it.

Lugh held out an arm to stop me, and then cocked his head. "You're drawn to the spear."

"Yeah, I guess I am actually." I peered up at the five sharp points before lowering my gaze to the gleaming golden rivets. "Is that its power?"

"What do you mean?"

"The magic rolling off of it," I explained. "Does it have something to do with drawing people to it? And, on that note, is *your* power drawing people to you?"

"No one else is drawn to this spear, Moira," he said quietly. "In fact, they're terrified of it. Uisnech only moved it because he cares deeply for me. But it makes his skin crawl. It makes everyone's skin crawl."

"I don't understand," I whispered.

He frowned, confusion rippling across his face. "You don't?"

My hands clenched. Suddenly, I didn't want to be doing this anymore. A dread had begun to seep into my bones, and warning bells clanged in my head. "What is this spear, Lugh? What's going on?"

Lugh crossed the room without another word and unlocked the case. The door hung open, and the gleaming gold winked at me.

"This spear," he began, staring at it with a strange expression on his face, "is part of me. And I am part of it. We're linked in a way that is almost impossible to understand, though I will try my best to explain it."

"It's part of you?" I whispered.

"My fae power is skill with a spear, but this particular weapon goes beyond that. When I use it, my powers are far greater than anything else most have ever seen. That's why the fae ran from me when I caught them attacking you in Mag Mell. It would strike them down. It would steal the breath from their lungs and the blood from their vein if I touched them with it."

Fear shuddered through me.

"But there is a downside to my powers, which is why I keep my spear locked up and hidden from those who wish to steal it from me." Lugh reached out and wrapped his hand around the spear, slamming the shaft onto the floor by his feet.

In an instant, my world changed. Something inside my soul snapped tight. Magic rushed through me like a category five hurricane. Power crackled between Lugh and his spear, and the entire room was engulfed by it.

My heart pounded as I stared into Lugh's midnight eyes. Lips parted, I shook my head. The magic pulsing between us clenched tight in my gut, and a strange sensation swirled between us. His power pummelled through my heart, but my own magic rushed right back toward him.

Fear tripped through me. I'd heard about this before.

I knew what it was.

"No!" I clutched at my heart and backed away from him, shaking my head in horror. "No, no, no."

"What is it?" Confusion and alarm flashed across his face. "What's wrong? I thought my spear did not scare you."

"You're my mate," I whispered. "You're my actual mate."

He shook his head, still confused. "Of course I am. Didn't you know? Didn't you feel the bond snap between us the moment we met? If not then, the moment in the training room?"

That moment he'd looked at me and laughed about the cruelty of fate.

"No." Closing my eyes, I twisted away. I couldn't bear to look at him anymore, not knowing the truth about our bond. Lugh Tuireann was my mate. The prophecy roared in my head, drowning out a moment that should have been one of the happiest of my life.

The King of Wraiths was my mate.

Which meant I would kill him one day.

18

I tore out of the castle. Now that I knew the truth, I couldn't stay here anymore. Every moment I spent with Lugh was another moment when I might stab him in the heart.

He caught my arm as I shoved my feet into my boots. "Moira, you have to explain what's going on. I realise it's an intense moment, finding your mate, but I honestly thought you already knew. All these times we've touched, I could feel it in my gut."

Tears stung my eyes. I kept my gaze on my boots. I couldn't look at him anymore. "Saoirse isn't the first druid I've met. There's another. Her name is Caer."

"I've heard of Caer," he said suspiciously, dropping my arm. "She tends to deal in prophecies that are a matter of life and death."

"Exactly." I tightened my laces and headed for the door. Then I stopped, twisting to give him one last look. He stood tall beside his harp, a piercing reminder that he was brutal and fierce but also soft, caring, and heartachingly perfect. I wanted to memorise his face. It would be the last time I ever saw it. Midnight blue hair, fierce black eyes, sharp curving horns, and cheekbones that could cut glass. Hands that were strong enough to pummel foes but soft enough to make me melt.

I closed my eyes. "Caer told me that I will one day kill my mate. I don't understand how it happened, but it turns out that's you. That's why I have to leave."

I was a warrior. I loved to fight. My blood sang when battle called. I'd always needed someone the same. I understood that now. I should have known from the moment I met Lugh that he would be my mate. We mirrored each other in a way that I could scarcely believe.

And that was why I had to leave.

With that, I pushed out the door and raced toward the castle gates. I wasn't sure if he would try to stop me when the shock of my words wore off, but I didn't want to stick around to find out. Instead, I clambered over the gates and dropped onto the ground on the other side. The guards shouted at me, but they didn't hold me back. They weren't there to keep us from leaving. They were there to keep enemies out.

And now I was one.

The city spread out before me, but the glittering

lights had faded as the moon stalked toward the horizon. It was the middle of the night. Most places were shut tight until morning. No trains ran this late, which meant I was kind of stuck. For now, I'd have to find a pub and crash for the night, until I could leave the next morning.

Time to go home. My heart squeezed. When I'd left London, I'd ached to stay, and now the very opposite was true. I didn't want to go back.

A few pubs on a street just off the High Street had their lights still blazing through the windows. I picked one called A Knight's End and pushed inside. A little bell clanged as I sauntered over to the bar, dropped onto the stool, and sunk my elbows onto the sleek wood.

"Rough night?" the bartender asked through a beard that could rival the thickest brush. His sandy hair matched, thick and hanging down to his shoulders. He wore a black t-shirt with a reaper illustration, and he had a tattoo on his arm of some sort of Celtic symbol.

"You have no idea," I muttered. How could I explain to a human that I'd found my mate and that I could never see him again? Because of a prophecy. From a druid. Who had originally come from the magical land called Faerie. He probably wouldn't serve me a drink.

"What's your poison?" he asked, flipping a shot glass in his beefy hands.

"Give me a shot of your best whiskey." I twisted

on my seat to see the vacancy sign flashing just outside the window. "You have some open rooms?"

"Sure." He poured the drink and slid the glass toward me. "Three hundred quid a night."

I made a face.

He let out a low chuckle. "Sorry. Prime real estate right here. Views of the castle, a one-minute walk to the Royal Mile. Tourists love it here. Plus, we have a special deal with Mary King's Close. Guests here enjoy free entry, and we do private tours every day at noon. Though tomorrow's already booked up."

Ah, Mary King's Close, the most famous close in all of Edinburgh. Once, it had been part of the Royal Mile, a bustling main street for businesses and homes. Over the years, the close had been built on top of, again and again until it was buried beneath the city. The area had been sealed shut. No sunlight, no fresh air, and no escape for plague victims. A lot of people had died in that close, and what humans didn't know now was that over half of them had been due to hungry vampires.

"So you charge extra for being near a veritable graveyard." I downed the shot and winced as fire burned my throat.

He shrugged. "Tourists are convinced supernatural shit is going down in there, especially after all those weirdos came out of the closet. You know some of them live in the castle on the hill? All this time, I thought the place was shut to visitors because the military was doing super secret training in there, but it turns out a fae king bought the damn place. Can you believe it?"

I swallowed hard. I was not yet ready to be reminded of the mate I'd left behind. "I heard the fae help keep the vampires in line."

He grunted. "They're all the same to me. Vampires, fae, werewolves. Did you know there are also magicians out there?"

"Sorcerers," I corrected.

"Yeah, sorcerer magicians." His grin widened. "A friend of mine bought this pretty cool drug off a magician the other day. It's called sapphire blue or something. And lemme tell you, that thing was poooooooootent."

My head jerked up. "Oh yeah? You got a name for this guy?"

The bartender jerked his head back and forth. "Nah. I just know he deals out of Mary King's Close but not at this time of night. You'd have to catch him during the day. But it's hard to get to him. Other than the tours, that place is shut to the public. I don't know how he manages."

Right. Of course he did. My mind ran a hundred miles an hour. If I could talk to the sorcerer, maybe I could find out which fae he'd sold drugs to, and then we could get a lead on who took Saoirse. I needed to get out of this town, for Lugh's sake, but I could check things out tomorrow before I got on the train.

"I've got some weed, though, if you'd like that instead?"

"No, thanks. I think I'll take another shot, and then head up to bed."

"You got it," he replied, pouring the drink before I could start babbling about fae mates and kings and evil prophecies. He didn't seem too keen on supernaturals, and I needed a room. Best to keep mum about the whole thing. Like Lugh preferred to do. Lugh. My mate.

Argh! I couldn't think about anything without my mind circling right back to his silky hair and perfect biceps.

I downed the shot and decided I should probably call it a night. Two whiskeys and my head already buzzed. The bartender tossed me a set of keys and instructed me to head to the third floor, first room on the right.

As I pushed up the stairs, the door to the pub opened, and a wave of cold air rushed inside. The little bell clanged, and the murmur of voices drowned it out. Huh. Guessed I wasn't the only living thing out there wandering the streets in need of a drink at two in the morning. The place was called A Knight's End, after all.

But something stopped me from finishing the trek up the stairs.

I wasn't entirely sure what set off the alarm bells. Something about the way the air moved as the new arrivals whispered through the bar. No. It wasn't that at all. It was the way they smelled. Lavender, iron, and dead leaves.

My heart dropped. It was the crew from the night of the attack in Mag Mell.

Gripping the banister, I eased into a crouch to see into the pub, but my view was blocked by the half-shut door.

"Yeah, can we have a round of bourbon? Here's a little extra for you to find something interesting in your stock room back there. We have some business to attend to out here. Trade secrets and the lot."

"Yeah, all right." The bartender's voice sounded pleasantly surprised. They must have passed him a tidy sum to make him vanish. At least they hadn't decided to kill him for his trouble. A moment later, footsteps thudded on the hardwood, and a door slammed shut.

"Ugh, humans." The female's voice dripped with disdain. The leader. The one who had the magic sword. "I'm so sick of having to pretend to care about them. Can't talk about supernatural stuff in their presence. It's time this world had a change."

"Nemain will make certain that our lives are for the better once she returns from the underworld," a quiet male voice replied. "Patience, Fiona."

I frowned. Nemain would change the world all right. She would make sure the humans of the world were her slaves, and she'd destroy every other supernatural race. I couldn't believe that there were other fae out there who wanted the same thing.

"It's been weeks," Fiona whined. "We've got the cauldron. Why won't it work?"

So we'd been right. The Cauldron Tossers had gotten their hands on the magical item, but they had no idea how to use it. That was a good sign, though their next words sent a chill down my spine.

"It won't work because we don't have his spear," the quiet male continued. "The prophecy girl said we needed to get it. I asked her again today, and she confirmed."

Prophecy girl. Saoirse. My heart flipped over. She was okay. She was still alive. And they were making her do prophecies for them just like we'd feared.

And we were back to that damn spear again.

"No matter," the male sniffed. "According to my source, Lugh is alone tonight, unguarded. His spear has been hidden away, which means he cannot use it against us. His little goblin is busy with another task. We'll take him tonight."

Wait. I leaned forward and the bannister creaked beneath me.

"I don't understand," Fiona said. "I thought we needed his spear."

"The prophecy made it clear we need something potent, which Lugh's spear is. But if his spear is potent, he will be, too. That weapon and him… they're attached somehow. We will sacrifice the king in order to get Nemain back."

My heart roared as the enemy's words echoed in

my mind. I'd left Lugh alone back at the castle, and Uisnech was off feasting on...whatever hobgoblins feasted upon. The guards were in place at the gates, but would they be able to stop this attack?

"Ooh, sacrifice the king," another voice said, cackling. "I love the sound of that. Let's hit him while he's asleep. He'll never see us coming."

19

I paced the warped floor in the pub's rented room. My hands clenched and then unclenched. Shaking my head, I tried to solve a puzzle that didn't seem to have an answer. These fae were going after Lugh. I needed to warn him, but...I couldn't risk being in his presence. What if I killed him?

Get a grip, I mentally shouted at myself. It wasn't like my arm would move in independence of my body. There might be a prophecy that I would kill him, but it wasn't like it would just come out of nowhere.

Right?

With a frustrated sigh, I punched a number into my cell. Lugh's number. Even if I couldn't go to him, I could warn him about what was coming his way. His phone rang and rang and rang. Swearing, I tried Uisnech next. If I couldn't warn Lugh himself, the hobgoblin was second best. He was out doing his feasting thing, but I was certain he would go back to the castle if it meant protecting Lugh.

But he didn't pick up his phone, either.

My mouth went dry as I tried to ignore what that meant. Best case scenario, Lugh was just asleep and Uisnech was still out on the town.

But my life didn't really work in best case scenarios.

I paced one more time and then nodded to myself. I was a warrior. Enough with the phone calls. Time to use my blade.

Patting my sword, I jogged down the stairs. If I couldn't warn Lugh, then I'd just have to fight the tossers here. Sure, making a war in a human establishment would bring unwanted attention onto the fae, but I didn't have any other choice. They had to be stopped before they attacked the castle.

"Where are they?" I barked when I flew into the pub like a frantic wraith. The bartender was back behind the wooden shelf again, collecting half a dozen discarded glasses, some three-quarters full. He was whistling to himself, but the sound cut off sharply when I thundered toward him.

He gave me a startled look. "Where is *who*?"

"The people who were in here earlier," I snapped. "The ones who gave you a tip to make yourself scarce."

"Oh." He narrowed his eyes in suspicion. "Were you eavesdropping?"

I rolled my eyes. "Yes. Now where are they?"

I didn't want to scare the shit out of a human, but I would if I had to. My hand twitched by my sword. Right now, it was hidden beneath my coat. But if I had to show 'ole Stabby to get him to talk, then so be it.

I'd done far worse things in my life than threaten a human.

"I don't know." He shrugged as if a sword-wielding fae wasn't standing right before him, ready to hurl her pointy knife at whoever crossed her next. "I poked out my head a few minutes ago to see if they wanted another drink, and they were gone."

"Bollocks!" I stormed toward the door, my coat flapping behind me.

"So, uh, you still want that room?" he called after me. "If not, I need the keys back!"

I answered by slamming the door in his face. Who has time for good manners when you have a realm to save from psychopaths?

Now where had those Cauldron Tossers gone? I whipped my head back and forth, glaring down one end of the street to the next. Nothing. Not even a dark silhouette melting into distant shadows. The fae could have gone anywhere in this city, and by the time I found them, they'd already have Lugh. If they didn't already.

I had only one choice. Well, I had two, but one was never going to happen. I could either forget about all this and go back home, liked I'd planned to originally. Or I could return to the castle and warn Lugh.

The castle twinkled in the distance. Clenching my hands, I went back.

~

Lugh was nowhere to be found inside the palace, and Uisnech was just as scarce. The guardhouse at the gate had been empty, which was a pretty ominous development, and I had no idea which rooms the twins lived in. So I found myself pounding on the only other fae's door I knew well enough to disturb in the middle of the night.

Imogen cracked open her door about a centimetre, her pink hair a curtain around her face. Sleepy eyes peered out at me. "Moira? Why are you knocking on my door at...?" She glanced behind her. "*Three AM?!*"

"I need your help," I hissed, all too aware of the many ears around the castle, not that anyone else would be awake right now. "There's been a plot against the king."

That woke her up.

Eyes suddenly alert, she flicked her gaze around the hallway behind me as if the plotters would appear there at any moment. "Plot against the king? How do you know? What's happening?"

"Can I come in?" I asked impatiently. "I really don't want to discuss this out here."

Even though there were few safe places to speak inside the castle, the rooms were at least warded enough that my voice wouldn't carry down the hallway. If our enemies were lurking right outside the door, sure, they'd hear every word. But if they decided to lurk outside this door, I'd show them my bloody blade.

Imogen opened the door wider, and I rushed inside. Her room was slightly larger than mine had been, with a similar bed, desk, and bedside table. But everything else had been transformed by pink. She had a fuzzy pink rug spread across the hardwood. Her bedspread was covered in pink flowers. Even her table lamp had been garnished with a pink shade.

"It has to do with my power," she said, chagrined. "I'm highly-attuned to colour. It communicates with me. Pink is the only thing that shuts it up."

"*Pink* shuts it up?" I asked, whirling to take in the very bright display of colour.

She nodded sagely. "You would think brown or black, right? But black is probably the loudest, and brown is one of those that kind of seeps into your skin."

"I..." In any other circumstance, I would want to sit down and quiz her on this very unique skill of hers. But I didn't really have time for that. "Interesting. Now listen to me. There's been a plot against the king, and someone has taken him. A lot of someones, actually."

"Does this have something to do with the attack earlier tonight?"

Had that really been tonight? I shook my head. So much had happened since then, it felt like days.

"Yeah, it was the same fae," I said quickly. "And I need your help. There was no one at the guardhouse when I came in, and I have no idea where Warin, Boudica, or the other warriors live."

She blinked at me, and then smiled. "You want me to find them for you."

"Or you could just tell me where they are." Before I could finish my sentence, my phone trilled. Sucking in a sharp breath, I slammed it against my ear without looking at the caller name.

"Hey, Moira." Kyle's easy voice slid over the line. Damn. My shoulders slumped. For a second there, I'd thought it was Lugh.

Out of the corner of my eye, I saw Imogen slip over to the door. I twisted toward her, and she pointed at the hallway and mouthed something about the warriors. She was going to go find them for me. I gave her a thumbs up and returned to my call.

"So I ran those faces through CCTV, and I got a few hits," he said.

Hope bloomed in my chest. "Are you serious? My god, Kyle. You're a lifesaver."

"Don't get too excited," he cut in. "We've got three faces, yeah? Well, I got their identities, but there are five known residences on file."

My hope got quickly squashed by the big bug known as reality. "Five."

While I couldn't deny Kyle had done great work and had finally dropped some leads on top of my head, five locations was four too many. The enemy wanted to murder Lugh. Tonight. And no telling what they would do with Saoirse now that they no longer needed her prophecies.

"Right," I grumbled. "Let's here them, then."

"Okay, the first location I think you can probably wipe off the board. It's the castle there on top of the hill."

"Makes sense. Some of them used to live here."

"The four others are all located throughout the city." The rustle of paper came over the line. "We've also got one in Bathgate, one in Leith, and one in Oxgangs. You have a pen and paper or should I text over the full addresses?"

"That was four." I furrowed my brows. "You said there were five."

"Oh, the fifth is another dead end like the castle. And that one doesn't even make sense. Mary King's Close. That place isn't even open to the public, is it?"

My heart skipped a beat. "Only for tours. Listen, Kyle. Can you just give me the address of the Mary King's Close one?"

The line was silent, other than the distant clacking of keys. "No, sorry. That's all it says. Mary King's Close. You really think that's the one?"

"Oh yeah. I'm certain of it." In fact, I would have bet a million quid on it. The bartender had mentioned humans being wary of supernatural activity in the close, and his friend had bought sorcerer drugs there as well. The pub even had a connection to the close, where those fae had turned up for drinks. They must be hiding out there. And they'd taken Saoirse and Lugh there, too.

Just as I hung up the call with Kyle, Imogen scurried back into the room, wringing her hands. "You get some kind of lead or something?"

"Yeah." I glanced behind her. "Where are the twins and the rest of the team? I know where they've taken the king."

"Oh good." She clapped her hands. "Are you going after him?"

"Yes, I am," I said, deciding it in an instant. I might be prophesied to kill him one day, but it wasn't going to be tonight. "But I need help from the rest of the team."

"They're grabbing their weapons and getting dressed. They said to tell you to get Lugh's spear and tell me where you want them to go. They'll meet you there."

I frowned. "Why do they want me to get the spear?"

She shrugged. "Something about his power.

How if you get it in the same room as him, then he'll be able to fight everyone off. I think he has some way of using it against lots of enemies at once. That's why it has five points instead of one like a normal spear. I'd go get it myself, but that thing freaks me out."

I thought back to what Lugh had told me about his spear—that it was a part of him, that the magic he could wield with it was terrifyingly fierce. About draining the blood from veins. If he was somehow trapped and we couldn't get to him, the spear might be the only thing that could get him out.

"Where should I tell them to meet you?" Imogen asked, cutting through my thoughts.

"Lugh is somewhere inside of Mary King's Close. The enemies have been hiding out in one of the buildings there, and that's where they'll have taken Lugh and Saoirse."

At least, I hoped they still had Saoirse. The alternative was too much to consider.

Imogen nodded. "I'll tell them to meet you at the entrance of the close. They've all been there before, on tours and things, so they'll know where to go. You go get the spear."

"Are you sure I shouldn't—"

"Listen, I've got this," she said. "I'll make sure they know where to go."

Without wasting any more time, I jogged out of the room and headed for the palace. It was so quiet inside. It didn't feel right without Lugh's presence echoing off the walls. Now that I knew the truth about our bond, I didn't understand how I hadn't seen it sooner. From day one, I'd felt his magic. I'd felt it pulse from his skin.

Shaking my head, I pressed the button beneath the shelf and watched the door swing inward. I darted down the hidden tunnel and came to a stop before the enclosed spear. My fingers twitched as I unlocked the case and pulled the spear into my hands.

My blood sang as I held it. Breath got caught in my throat. Everything inside of me felt weak, and I could practically feel Lugh's heartbeat in my palms. A tear slipped down my cheek, and I clenched the spear to my chest.

At least he was alive. The spear pulsed with his life-force, it rumbled with the strength of his soul. He probably couldn't feel me or hear me or sense me at all, but I felt the urge to speak to him all the same.

"I will get you out of this," I whispered fiercely. "And if they've harmed you, I will make them pay."

20

The door to Mary King's Close swung ominously in the winter wind, creaking on rusted hinges. Swallowing hard, I edged forward and peered down the dark alley. At one point in time, the close had been open to the public. You could descend into the depths of the ancient, smothered streets and take a look around. Now two large double doors blocked the way.

Or they normally did, anyway.

Right now, they were swinging on their hinges.

The team was meeting me here in twenty minutes. Imogen had shot me a text to say they were getting suited up for a fight, and they were having trouble finding all of their weapons. The Cauldron Tossers had stolen some, apparently.

Before I'd left the castle, I'd placed a note on the bookshelf, just in case Uisnech showed up to check on the spear. I didn't want the little guy to freak out when he found the king—and his special weapon—missing in action. I still hadn't been able to get ahold of him, the team were running late, and I was all alone down here with Lugh's gleaming spear catching the attention of everyone who passed by.

Taking another glance behind me, I ducked into the gloomy alley and edged the door shut with my boot. I could take a quick look around. From what I knew about the close, it was a maze that could take several hours to fully explore, so I might as well do a quick scout ahead to see what I could find.

I headed for the shadowy staircase that led me down to a street with no sky. Gloom quickly surrounded me, the only sound the distant drip of water on stone. The stone walls rose high on either side of me, angling together at the top. Between them hung old scraps of dull brown laundry. Part of the tour, a demonstration of what life must have been like centuries ago.

The stench of sewage and dust swirled into my nose as I crept along the tunnelled street. I passed boarded-up windows in buildings that would have been home to businesses that had tried to survive in the once bustling market. Fabric merchants, tobacco shops, restaurants. None of that was here anymore.

The street sloped upward, and I ducked through an archway where several low-ceilinged rooms led to the next street. In my hand, the spear began to hum, and I stopped short, heart racing.

The spear continued to buzz against my fingers,

and the golden rivets sparked with light. Biting the insides of my cheeks, I peered around the stone archway that led to the following street. There, in the distance, a faint light splashed onto the ground. It was the only light in the close other than the now-gleaming spear I carried with me.

That must be where the fae were hiding out.

Taking a deep breath, I tiptoed across the room and braced my back against the next wall. I waited, counting to ten in case they'd spotted me. When no one lurched out of the darkness, I did the same again. Peer, prance, hide.

Finally, I had nowhere else to go but into the middle of the street ahead. I closed my eyes and called upon all the courage I had inside of me. I didn't want to take on these fae alone, but I had to be sure that Lugh was here. Then the warrior team and I could make a solid plan of attack.

I leaned the spear against the wall so that it wouldn't give away my position. And then I inched my way into the street, doing my best to hug the shadows.

Slowly, I crept closer to the light. It was coming from a window on the ground floor, two buildings down. My boots scuffed against the ancient street as I edged ever closer. When I reached the building without incident, I pressed my back against the wall and ducked my head to look inside.

My eyes darted around. It was some kind of stop for the tour. There was an ancient glass-blowing display in the center, and long shelves of delicate glass hung along the walls.

And there they were. All of them. Eight fae dressed in black leather—we'd taken out a few already so this must be who was left. None of them wore masks, but I didn't recognise them. They were surrounding two forms hanging from the ceiling by rattling chains. My heart leapt into my throat. I'd found Saoirse and Lugh.

They both looked like they'd been through hell and back. Deep gashes slashed across their bodies and faces. Purple splotches circled red-tinged eyes. My hands clenched, and I swallowed a vicious growl.

How dare they.

The mating bond snapped tight, and Lugh's head suddenly jerked up. He met my eyes through the grimy window, his dark irises churning with dread. Frowning, he gave a quick shake of his head.

Unfortunately, that caused two problems. The first problem was this: I had no idea what he was shaking his head at. My presence here? Maybe. The fact I'd sauntered into the depths of Mary King's Close without any backup? Probably. The understanding that I was about to do something very, very stupid? Most definitely.

The second problem was...one of the Cauldron Tossers noticed Lugh's head shake and turned to stare right at me.

The black-clad male gave a shout, and the rest

of the enemies whipped my way. Well, there went my element of surprise. Three of them grabbed their swords from where they'd propped them against the wall and charged toward me.

Fortunately—because it wasn't all bad, just ninety percent—I was ready for them. I unsheathed my sword and swung hard at the first opponent to rush my way. The blade slashed right through his chest, killing him instantly. A part of me felt terrible for what I'd done, but then I saw Lugh hanging from chains out of the corner of my eye, one end wrapped tightly around his throat, and I didn't feel so terrible anymore.

The next two attackers came at me simultaneously. They swung in unison, which made their blows easy to dodge. I ducked low and then spun onto my back, holding my sword straight up. They both stumbled back, unsure of how to respond. And then I whirled to the side, slashing one right in the shin.

The enemy dropped his sword and hobbled back. "I surrender. Please don't kill me."

I grinned and jumped up, eyeing the second. He narrowed his eyes, but then his gaze flicked to his fallen comrade. His sword clattered to the stone. "Yeah, I think I'm good."

He rushed over to his friend and helped him hobble down the close.

Rolling back my shoulders, I strode through the open doorway where four more enemies blocked my path to Lugh and Saoirse. Behind them, the female leader, Fiona, flipped through a book and muttered to herself while waving her hands over a cauldron.

Gundestrup's Cauldron. My stomach flipped as I stared at it. The silver bowl-shaped vessel was probably as tall as my knees and just as wide. The sides were covered in six or seven uneven panels that were carved with images of animals and Celtic symbols. Its magic hummed, creating a strange, eerie song that caused tears to sting my eyes.

Fiona snapped the book shut, and then turned to me. She no longer wore a mask, and her brilliant blue eyes swept across me, smugness curving up her thin lips. She had yellow hair, kind of like mine, but it was dull and ashy instead of golden. "Look who it is. The mate of the nightmare wraith."

At the words *nightmare wraith*, my stomach dropped through the floor. Images of hooded figures flashed through my mind. Hands pinning me down, horrific screams ripping from my throat. I tightened my grip on my sword.

"I don't know what you're talking about." Which was honest. I didn't. Sure, I was Lugh's mate, but what did that have to do with nightmare wraiths? Those creatures of darkness and pain hadn't been seen in this realm for centuries, save for once. Most of them had never even come through the portal. They'd stayed in Faerie, according to legends.

"Your precious mate is a nightmare wraith,"

Fiona sneered, striding toward me. "Or did he not tell you?"

I flicked my eyes toward Lugh, who was avoiding my gaze. He kept his own eyes locked on his feet instead. Confusion rippled through me, as well as a heavy dose of fear. "Lugh is not a nightmare wraith."

Nightmare wraiths were creatures of the night, spectres of evil. They didn't have souls, and they didn't care about anything but feeding on the fear of everyone else. They chased you down, pinned you, and squatted on top, pouring horrifying images into your head.

They'd done it to me, once. When I'd been just a fae child, some nightmare wraiths had gone on a spree through the English countryside, terrorising everyone they met. It was the most horrifying thing that had ever happened to me, and I still had nightmares about them to this day.

But they'd been stopped. And none had been seen in this realm since.

"Oi, prophecy girl," Fiona snapped. "Tell the sword master the truth."

Saoirse sagged against her chains and sighed. "It's true, Moira, in a way. Lugh was once a nightmare wraith. In fact, he was the commander of an entire clan of them. Uisnech...helped him. He found a way to give Lugh a real life. But nightmare wraiths cannot have souls, so it couldn't reside in his own body. Uisnech found a way to put the soul in the spear and link the two of them together."

Shock hit me square in the gut. I stumbled backward, my mouth opening with soundless protests. This couldn't be real. It was some kind of trick, another trap to distract us from the truth.

But Fiona hadn't been the one to speak those words out loud.

Saoirse had. And Lugh was doing nothing to rebuke her.

"Lugh," I whispered as tears burned my eyes. I glanced across his face. That strong, fierce jaw. His cheekbones as high as the sky. The silken strands of midnight blue hair. He did not look like a nightmare wraith at all. "Is this true?"

"I tried to tell you earlier," he said tiredly. "I thought you would run screaming from me when you found out the truth. But it turns out, I didn't even have to tell you about my past to get you running."

Guilt tripped through me, even as horror churned in my gut.

Lugh—*my* Lugh—was a nightmare wraith.

"So, you terrorised people?" I stepped back toward the door. "You filled their minds with death and gore and horror? You *fed* on them?"

"Not since I've had my soul." He slumped even further against his bonds. "Not since Uisnech saved me."

Now it all truly did make sense. Why he felt

such a bond with the little hobgoblin. Why he'd made his Court the way he had. Why he felt the need to hide and save others that were lost. He was a fae—the nightmare wraiths were very much fae, but a different kind than the ones who were part of the Court—but he was one of the deadliest alive.

"So now you see why it's acceptable for his life to be a sacrifice for the greater good," Fiona said, cutting through my wheeling thoughts. "The magic of a wraith is powerful, particularly one who has been bound with a soul. We were going to use his spear to spark the magic of the cauldron, but that proved difficult to find."

My gut clenched, and my head shot up. "You want the spear instead of Lugh? I'll give it to you."

"No," Lugh growled, finally looking up to meet my eyes. "If they destroy the spear, I'll lose my soul. It's the only thing binding me to who I am now."

My heart thundered.

"And if I lose my soul," he continued, "I'll be the commander of wraiths once again. I won't be able to stop myself from ordering them to flee from Faerie and swarm this realm. I will *want* them to feed on everyone who lives here. Because I won't be *me* anymore. I won't be Lugh."

My entire body shuddered in response to his words. I'd faced a lot of things in my long life. The walking dead, vampires who wanted to rip me to shreds, murderous psychopaths who wanted to bury me alive. But his words sent a new terror through my soul.

If he brought the nightmare wraiths out of Faerie, they would swarm this realm and feast on every last human alive. No one would be safe.

Fiona clasped her hands together. "Oh dear. Looks like we really do need to sacrifice Lugh."

"No!" I sprang into action. Sword whirling, I aimed my attack right at her head. Her bodyguards jumped into place, and one of them took the hit instead. The male fell, blood spraying onto my black trousers.

Grimacing, I turned to the next. They all rushed me, and my instincts took over. I sliced to the right, and the next one fell. Another lurched toward me, and I ducked low. When he was busy recovering from his attempt, I lunged forward. The blade sank into his chest.

Two more were left, not including Fiona, who was back to muttering at the cauldron again. She'd grabbed a small dagger and was slicing it through the air in some kind of pattern. It was a ritual, one that obviously required blood and deep, dark magic. She was two seconds away from sacrificing Lugh, and I had to stop her.

Without pausing a beat, I dropped my sword. My hands slung toward my hidden blades. I grabbed two in one hand, and one in the other. Closing my eyes, I let my magic pour through my veins. I could feel my enemy's weapons whistling closer.

And then I threw.

The two in my left hand sank into the bodyguards.

And the one in my right slammed right into Fiona's neck.

They all fell. Blood painted the floor.

The sight of it made me sick, and my stomach turned. But I shook off my dread and rushed over to Saoirse and Lugh. Within seconds, I'd undone their chains. Lugh's dark eyes met mine, and my entire body hummed with the need to launch into his arms.

But then something sounded from behind me.

Lugh's entire body went rigid. His eyes darkened. A growl slipped from his throat.

I turned. One of the enemies who'd fled was back.

And he had Lugh's spear.

21

The male fae's smile stretched wide as he held the spear up before him. "Don't want to forget about this old thing here, do you?"

"Give me the spear, Eoin," Lugh growled, inching forward so that his front now pressed against my back. Just the feel of him this close to me made my body sigh with relief. And then I remembered we were staring down the enemy. And that enemy had Lugh's soul in his hands.

Wait a minute. Eoin? My eyes widened. I knew that name. He had been the fae that very first night in the courtyard when I'd been spying and had overheard Lugh asking someone about the cauldron. He must have turned on Lugh sometime after that.

"What would happen if I snapped this thing in half?" Eoin snarled, spinning the spear in his hands so that it now sat horizontal on his palms. His long fingers curled around the shaft. My heart stopped.

"Moira, get down on your knees," Lugh ordered. "Saoirse, too."

Eoin sniggered. "Yeah, they should get down on their knees where they belong."

I wanted to punch the guy in the throat for that, but I listened to Lugh instead. I didn't know what propelled me to trust him, but I ducked down, knees and hands slamming hard against the rough stone ground. Saoirse did the same by my side, even though she was practically unconscious at this point.

The spear hummed as soon as I hit the ground. Magic vibrated through the underground close, the walls rocking as deep tremors caused glasses and bowls to tumble from the shelves and crash onto the floor.

I glanced up just in time to catch the flash of surprise on Eoin's face. The spear ripped out of his hands with a deadly force, and Eoin's body flew backward out the door. The spear landed in Lugh's hands, the vibrating intensity knocking hard against my ears.

I swore they even popped.

"Come on," Lugh growled. "Let's get out of here. The walls are crumbling. This place could cave in."

To emphasise his point, another glass shattered right beside my foot, and shards scattered everywhere. One sharp sliver even dug its way into my arm.

"Ow." I jumped up, wrapping my hands around

Saoirse's arms and pulling her with me. She stumbled a bit, her body still broken from the terror the enemies had put her through.

A chunk of wall slammed onto the floor beside us. Lugh pushed me forward, and I broke out into a half-jogging run, doing my best to support Saoirse's weight. We rushed into the close, turning right to zoom straight for the exit.

But ten more black-clad figures whispered out of the shadows, led in front by—

My stomach dropped. Imogen's pink hair stood out from the rest. Her eyes flashed; her grin twisted in a way I'd never seen before. I glanced from her delighted face to the black-clad fae that surrounded her. They all held blades, including her, though hers was a bright, neon pink. I shook my head, taking a step back, still holding tight to Saoirse.

"Imogen, what the hell are you doing?" I demanded. "What did they tell you to get you to join them?"

She laughed, and then rolled her eyes. "They didn't have to tell me anything. I've been one of them all this time. How do you think they learned everything they did about the Court? I can't believe you thought my power had something to do with my love for pink. My *real* gift is the ability to blend into the shadows. No one ever knows I'm there. How do you think I became such a good thief?"

She snapped her fingers, and she vanished

before my eyes. She came back into view almost instantaneously.

I shook my head, and she continued.

"You were such a prat to come to me about Lugh. If you hadn't, you might have actually saved him. But there are more of us Athaira loyals than you thought, and they were ready to charge in when I told them you were here."

Everything suddenly made sense. How the enemies had known so much about our every move. Why Saoirse's vision had been muddied about someone with red hair—it had been *pink* hair all along. And Imogen must have overheard the details about the back gates, and that was how she'd let the traitors into the castle.

I jumped when another chunk of rock slammed into the ground behind us. Glancing up at Lugh, my heart pounded. The close was caving in on itself, and we were surrounded by a dozen enemies.

"What do we do?" I whispered to my mate, hoping he heard me beneath the rumble of the earth. Power still sparked across his skin. The magic he'd called upon to bring his spear to himself had caused the avalanche, but there was nothing he could do to stop it now.

He glanced up at the shifting floor above us. "We're going to have to fight."

"What about Saoirse?" I asked. "She's unconscious, Lugh."

"I'll take Saoirse," a voice called from behind us.

I whirled toward the new arrival, and my heart tripped when Uisnech whispered out of the darkness, Boudica, Warin, and ten other warriors following just behind him. His eyes flashed as they met mine, and he gave me a solemn nod. "I got your note."

"Thank the Morrigan," I muttered.

"Let's not go that far," Uisnech chattered. He scurried toward me and took Saoirse in his little green arms. As soon as he'd pulled her back, the warrior team strode in and formed a V behind me and Lugh.

Sucking in a deep breath, I turned and grinned at Imogen. "Well, looks like you're not the only one who knows how to call for backup."

With a high-pitched scream, she raced toward us, blade raised over her head like something out of a horror film. I whisked two hidden daggers from my vest and hurled them through the air. They thunked into the armoured bodies of the two closest attackers. Blood spread from the wounds, but they didn't slow the fae down.

The close erupted into chaos. Warriors beside me flew into battle, and Lugh wielded his spear. I grabbed two more daggers and held my ground, waiting for the enemy to come closer. One rushed toward me, dark hair hidden beneath a black cap, orange eyes flashing with rage. He held two swords, and they spun like a whirlwind of pain.

He sliced them toward me, but I danced back. I

threw a dagger, and it hit him square in the head. He thunked to the ground, revealing another enemy hidden behind him. She had fierce, shortly-cropped purple hair, and she was holding a bow and arrow.

With a gasp, I ducked down just in time to feel the whistle of the arrow soar over my head. A loud crunch echoed from behind me as it sank into one of my friends. Gritting my teeth, I glanced behind me to find one of the warriors who'd been guarding Saoirse now down on the ground.

Uisnech's little green ears twitched in fear, and then he pulled Saoirse further into the shadows.

The ranger drew another arrow, and I flattened myself on the ground before rolling to the side. The arrow skittered off the stone and ricocheted into the air. Out of the corner of my eye, I could see Lugh whirling, spear sparking with electric energy.

A rock slammed into the ground by my face.

Heart hammering, I looked up. The ground above us had cracked. Any minute now, and we'd all be toast. We had to get out of here.

"A way has opened back here!" The hobgoblin's screech came shooting through the chaos.

"Retreat!" I jumped to my feet and screamed the words at my comrades. "The close is caving in! Retreat!"

Twisting on my feet, I rushed back to hook my arm around Saoirse's waist. Uisnech looked up at me, green eyes spread wide.

"You've got her other side?" I demanded.

He nodded. "Yes, my noble friend."

"Come on. Let's get out of here." I pushed forward. Saoirse dangled helplessly between us, but we inched away from the fight in a hasty retreat. As I glanced behind us, I could still see the warriors fighting. They were protecting our retreat, taking down the enemy one by one as the walls literally fell on top of their heads.

Uisnech pointed at the crack that had formed in the walls. A dim light speared the hole, a beacon of safety amidst the doom.

And then a figure rose out of the darkness. Fiona and her ashen hair, her eyes alight with fire. She grinned as she raised her arms. Magic crackled, bouncing across her skin like lightning.

The three of us came to a sudden stop, and Uisnech let out a little shriek.

I let go of Saoirse. Uisnech took her weight, and then I angled my body in front of them, blocking them from Fiona's view.

"When you try to kill a fae," the female said, lightning crackling up to the thundering floor, "you should know her power, her skill. Every time a blade swings through the air, it gives me power. So you and every other idiot fae in this close have only charged my magic. And look at me now."

She was charged all right. Bright white sparks shot along her arms and legs, burning up her clothes as they went. Her hair was alight with her power. It swirled in the air like strands of pure lightning.

"Move out of my way, Morrigan lover, or I will *make* you move." Her voice was low, quiet, dangerous.

But I was pretty damn dangerous myself.

"Duck low, hobgoblin," I whispered urgently, my heart hammering against my ribs. I had no idea if this was going to work, but I had to trust my gut. I had to trust my mate.

Uisnech let out a little chirp. I knew without looking that he had fallen face-first onto the ground and that he had taken Saoirse along with him.

Fiona cocked her head when I held my hand out to my side. "Whatever do you think you're doing, Morrigan lover?"

"You'll see. But you should come up with a better insult than that. You're just reminding me of why I fight." I curled my hand into trembling claws and braced my core. Power flickered around me, just slightly, as I ground my teeth. The magic from Lugh's spear rippled toward me, but then it vanished just as fast.

Pulling a deep breath in through my nose, I parted my lips and whispered, "Lugh."

The bond between us snapped tight, and suddenly his eyes were on my back. The power of his nightmare wraith shot toward me, and I gasped as it slammed hard into my soul. Wind whipped my hair, and a thousand tiny strands of fire licked up from the ground to surround me.

"What's going on?" Fiona narrowed her eyes, and her own magic became a crackling storm around her body. "Stop it right now!"

The wind grew stronger and stronger around my hand, and then suddenly, something solid slammed into my palm. I closed my fingers around it and grinned, twisting it sideways so that the five points were now aimed right at her chest.

"Lugh's spear." Fiona's eyes widened. "But you can't. No one can wield it but him."

"Oh, but *I* can."

She screamed and launched toward me with her lightning magic hurtling straight at my heart. I pulled back the spear and threw, putting all of my fae strength behind it. It soared through the air, the glistening tips flashing with magic.

It collided with Fiona, and her body buckled, curling around the points. Blood sprayed the rubble. Magic flashed through the rumbling close, the lightning vanishing in a cloud of black dust. The world went eerily silent.

Uisnech stepped up to my side and peered down at the fae's broken body. Her lifeless eyes stared up at the crumbling ceiling.

"Is that it, my noble friend?" he asked.

I cupped my hand around his face, my heart aching. "That's it, Uisnech. For now."

22

The small room on the top floor of the residential halls lacked a working heating system, but I was somehow going to miss that bone-deep chill when I went south. Most of my belongings had been burnt after the Sapphire bomb went off in my original room, but I found a few things to pack in my bag anyway.

The very act of folding a shirt and putting it in the satchel gave me the closure to know that I'd made the right choice.

Probably.

I kept going back and forth about it.

On the one hand, this was not my Court and Lugh was not my king. I'd pledged myself to Clark, and that hadn't changed, no matter what had happened since I'd arrived in Edinburgh. She needed me, and truth be told, I didn't want to lose her friendship. Not to mention the whole prophecy part of it all. Lugh, the King of Wraiths, was my mate, and I was destined to kill him.

Kind of a hard thing to get past.

On the other hand, *Lugh was my mate*. I ached to stay by his side. I wanted to curl up in his arms. I wanted to feel his lips on my skin. I wanted to fight by his side and face down his enemies.

With a sigh, I wrapped my sword in the black cloth and gave it a pat.

This had been one wild ride. After I'd defeated Fiona with Lugh's spear, Imogen and the rest of her band of Cauldron Tossers had thrown up their white flag and had surrendered. Both sides had lost warriors in the battle, but in the end, they'd lost more.

Lugh and his team had gathered them up and then deposited them in the castle prison. I wasn't entirely sure what he would do with them now, but that wasn't my business. Not anymore. I'd done my part. Mostly. I'd helped stop them from bringing Nemain back from the dead.

The only problem was...the cauldron had, as far as we could tell, been buried in the close. We'd only managed to get everyone out before the whole thing caved in, transforming Edinburgh's city centre into a whole load of rubbish.

It was going to take a long time for them to sort that out, and Lugh had donated a large portion of his massive wealth to help the city. He would oversee it as much as possible and get his hands on the cauldron as soon as it was found.

And now I was needed back in London.

I shouldered my bag and trailed down the stairs, trying to find an excuse to slow my exit. The training room. Obviously, I needed to say goodbye to everyone there. When I reached the ground floor, I hung a left and entered the building just opposite the halls.

Inside, the twins were training. They were a rush of speed and agility, almost exactly matched in skill. Boudica whirled and pinned Warin to the ground. Like I said. *Almost* exactly.

Warin glanced past her, pushed her away, and jumped to his feet. "Moira! That looks like a bag. Does that mean you really are leaving us?"

"I'm afraid so." I edged into the training room and looked around, smiling at the various weapons that adorned the walls. It was too bad I'd never had a chance to train in this room. It would have been fun. "I'm needed back at Court. Werewolf problems. I'm sure you get it."

It was only a little white lie. Clark was having werewolf problems, like always, but she'd told me to take my time. When I'd told her everything about Lugh—the nightmare wraiths, the mating bond— she'd been far more understanding than I'd expected. I thought she'd be upset that one of her closest confidantes had mated with the enemy, but her soft voice had soothed all those fears away.

"If he's your mate, he can't be all that bad," she had said on the phone. "You can stay there with him as long as you'd like, you know. Take your time. Do what you need to do, Moira. It's your life. Not mine."

"But the prophecy..." I'd tried to say.

"Prophecies can be changed. They can be broken. Look at me and Balor. Caer tried to tell us that our love would destroy the world."

Clark had a point. Prophecies were only prophecies, not facts. They were things that *could* happen. Not things that would.

Still, I didn't want to chance it.

"Earth to Moira," Boudica said with a laugh, snapping her fingers in front of my eyes. "Where'd you go, darling?"

"Sorry." I shook my head. "It's been a long-ass week."

She chuckled. "Tell me about it. I love a good fight, but I could use a week in the sun to decompress from all that stress."

I grinned back. "You know you can visit London anytime. It's no beach, but it's warmer than here."

"Maybe." She slung her arm around my neck and gave me a quick hug. "As long as you can promise that your queen won't try to make us join her Court. I know it's unorthodox here, but it's home."

I gave a nod. Clark and I hadn't really had that chat yet, but I knew I'd be able to make her understand. She and Lugh could form some sort of alliance. One that would allow him to continue as he was, as long as he did not challenge her throne.

With one last hug, I backed out of the training room and headed to the healing ward. Inside, I found Saoirse awake and smiling. Beside her sat the hobgoblin. He'd barely left her side since the whole ordeal. The poor creature had been worried sick about her, and I no longer understood why I hadn't been a big fan of Uisnech when I first met him.

He wasn't like other hobgoblins. Not that I'd actually met very many.

This time, though, he wasn't too pleased to see me. He narrowed his green eyes at my bag and scowled. "No. You cannot. Noooooooope!"

"Uisnech," I sighed, dropping by bag by Saoirse's healing ward door. "Please stop. I don't want to leave with you angry at me."

"Then you shouldn't leave, now should you?" he snapped.

"Uisnech," I said again. "I can't stay."

"You know you will be leaving me with a very grumpy king. I do not appreciate having to deal with Lugh's tantrums in your absence." He looked away and sniffed very dramatically.

"Frankly, I don't think he's the one being grumpy in this situation." Smiling, I dropped down on the chair next to him, and took his little hand in mine. "Hey. Please don't hate me. I have to go, but I promise I'll see you again."

He glanced back, his eyes shining. "You will?"

"Of course. You and I have a bond now. We survived a battle together. That means something."

"Is that a noble warrior thing?" he asked, his voice hitching at the end.

I grinned. "That's right. The way you helped Saoirse, you're a noble warrior now. Which means you need to understand why I must go. I know you're not a fan of the Morrigan, but she's my friend, and she's my queen. I need to go home, Uisnech."

With a heavy sigh, he gave a grudging nod. "As a fellow noble warrior, I understand your plight. But you cannot leave here forever. I am going to take you at your word. When Lugh needs you again, I will call on you."

"It's a deal," I said before flicking my eyes to Saoirse. She'd been watching the entire exchange with a bemused expression on her face. "You're looking better."

"The healers have made me as good as new. I can go back to my room any time now, but I'm enjoying the extra attention. And food. So I'll spend another night here." Her purple eyes shone, but they still had that haunted look about them.

When we'd finally had a chance to speak to Saoirse about what had happened, we'd learned that the enemy had treated her like a prisoner of war. They had tortured her for information and demanded she give them a prophecy. At first, she'd resisted, but then she'd given in. None of us blamed her for that. When she finally managed a single prophecy for them, she'd discovered that intense, all-consuming magic was needed as a sacrifice for the cauldron. Lugh's spear would do.

The details of her exact prophecy she'd kept mum. She said it didn't matter anymore. We'd stopped it from coming true.

As I turned to go, she grasped my hand and clung tight. "You can change your destiny, Moira. Don't forget that."

"I know." Tears filled my eyes. "There's always that chance, but I can't risk it. I've lost too many people. I won't lose him, too."

~

I dragged my feet toward The Royal Palace. I had no more excuses. No more fae to speak to before I left. Sure, I could walk along the cobblestones and trail my fingers across the Great Hall's majestic tables one last time. I could poke my head into the kitchen and say goodbye to Selma, not that she cared.

But it was time now for me to face Lugh. One final time.

With a deep breath, I strode to the door and pushed it open. As soon as I stepped foot inside, my ears were met with that haunting melody. He was playing the harp again, the strands of music swirling through the hallways like a strange, dark magic I wanted to pull into my bones.

The harp stopped suddenly, and Lugh appeared in his arched doorway, his dark hair ruffled, his shirt nowhere to be seen. I swallowed hard as I took in his washboard abs and sculpted cheekbones. Instead of running away from this, I wanted to launch into his arms.

I set my bag on the floor and shifted awkwardly on my feet.

"You've come to say goodbye." He disappeared back into his rooms, leaving his door hanging open.

He wasn't going to make this easy on me then. Fair enough.

With a deep breath, I squared my shoulders and edged into his rooms. The place was a wreck, far more so than usual. Books had been tossed about with abandon. Dirty plates were stacked in the kitchen. The floor was covered in soot.

I lifted a brow. "Um. Did someone break in here again?"

"No." His voice was cold as he turned his back on me. "Say what you have come here to say, Moira."

"Lugh," I pleaded.

He kept his back turned toward me and strode over to the window.

"Lugh. Please. It doesn't have to be this hard." I took a step toward him and then paused.

"No, it doesn't," he said quietly. "For one, you

could stay here with me. I am your mate. We belong together, not apart."

"I told you about the prophecy. It said that I'll—"

"Fuck the prophecy," he growled, whipping toward me. "The prophecy doesn't matter. All that matters is how I feel about you and how you feel about me. Tell me, Moira." He strode toward me, his dark power whorling through the room like a tornado. "Do you want to kill me?"

I blinked up at him, my voice stuck in my throat.

"Tell me the truth," he demanded. "Tell me you want to stab your blade into my heart."

My hands clenched. "Of course I don't. I've never wanted that. I don't understand how I ever could."

He grabbed my hands and pulled me to his chest. "Then stay."

"I can't," I said, tears springing into my eyes. "The idea that I could kill you terrifies me. I won't risk it. I won't. I refuse to put you in harm's way, especially when that harm is *me*."

"But it's just a prophecy." He closed his eyes and breathed me in. Heat sparked in my gut, and I found myself pressing closer to him, letting my head fill with the burning scent of him, that fire and mist and pine. It was hard to care about what might happen at some point way into the future when he was right here in front of me now.

"Prophecies," I said slowly, "predict the future.

They don't always come true, but most of the time, they do."

Breath shuddering from his lungs, Lugh stepped back, hands still clutched tightly to mine. His dark eyes flicked across my face, drinking me in. "I just need to know one thing, and I need you to tell me the truth. You tell me this, and I'll let you go."

My heart thumped, and I nodded.

He sucked in a deep breath and clenched his jaw. "You have a fear of the nightmare wraiths. I can sense it in you. You've encountered us—*them* —before."

My hands instinctively tightened around his as that familiar fear pounded through me. "Yes. They attacked me when I was young."

He shook his head sadly. "That is the true reason you are leaving, is it not? You are frightened by what I am, by what I once was. You learned the truth of me, and you want to flee."

"Lugh," I whispered, staring up at him. "Look into my eyes and ask yourself if you really believe that's the truth. You know it isn't. The nightmare wraiths, they terrify me, but that's not what you are now. I've seen you for who you are, and you are not the nightmares that have plagued me. *You are mine.*"

His eyes flashed, and he wrapped his strong arms around my body, resting his chin on the top of my head. I squeezed my eyes tight, hugging him back. We stood there like that for what felt like hours. He held me, and I held him, and we pretended that a world existed where we could stay in each other's arms forever.

Best case scenario, I could stay and we would find a way to avoid the prophecy from ever coming true. I would be happy, and he would be, too. We could have little wraith babies and sit in the Great Hall laughing and drinking with the rest of the Court. As we stood there like that, I imagined this whole life, stretching out for years and years ahead of us.

But there was a worst case scenario, too. One I would never forget. Somehow, I would kill him. I couldn't imagine how it could come to pass now, but I didn't doubt that it could.

When he pulled back, he rubbed his thumb across my jaw and gave me a sad smile. "Is there any way at all I can convince you to stay here with me?"

"No, Lugh," I whispered. "There really isn't. Not now, anyway. Just give me some time. I will search for a way to change this. Maybe there's a magic out there that can make the prophecy untrue."

"Okay, then." He sighed, leaned down, and gave me one last lingering kiss. I melted against him, memorising the feel of his lips against my skin. Our bond snapped tight, coming to life at our touch. It would always be a part of me, no matter how far I ran.

Slowly, I edged down the hallway toward the

front door. I grabbed my bag and slung it over my shoulder. For a moment longer, I just stood there staring at him.

"Would you like me to walk you to the train station?" he asked. "Or drive you? I have a fleet of cars that rarely gets used."

"I think," I said slowly, "that if I spend another moment with you then I'll talk myself out of what I'm doing."

A slight smile tipped up the corners of his mouth. "Don't tempt me to trap you here for another night. You know Uisnech would gladly help fit the lock on your door."

I laughed. "I'm surprised he hasn't already tried."

And then the smile died on my lips. This was it, then. I couldn't stall any longer. With one last longing glance in his direction, I twisted on my feet and left The Royal Palace behind.

I could feel his eyes on me until I'd passed through the gates, and even as far as the end of the Castle Esplanade. I had come here to trap him, to take him back in chains to my queen. Instead of all that, I was leaving with my soul eternally attached to his, and my heart pretty much cleaved in two. I'd long ago accepted that I would never live a happy life with a mate, but I hadn't known what that truly meant until now.

It sucked. Like, really, really bad.

Boots scuffing the cobblestone, I paused and

glanced over my shoulder. The castle loomed above, the lights twinkling through the heavy clouds. Even from a distance, I felt the pull of Lugh. I couldn't sever the bond between us no matter how hard I tried.

And I didn't need a prophecy to know that I couldn't stay away from him forever.

AUTHOR'S NOTE

Many of the settings in this book are based on real locations in Edinburgh. Castle Wraith, for example, is Edinburgh Castle in the real world. The layout for the buildings is based on the current map of the castle, and many of the descriptions match, such as details about the Great Hall and the Castle Esplanade.

Mary King's Close is very much a real location. Centuries ago, it was a bustling street full of merchants and markets, but it was "buried" as buildings kept expanding upward. Plague victims were indeed trapped inside. It's now a popular attraction with guided tours. I highly recommend visiting!

Demons After Dark: Temptation

Sinful Touch

Darkest Fate

Hellish Night

ABOUT THE AUTHOR

Jenna Wolfhart spends her days dreaming up stories about swoony fae kings and rugged blacksmiths. When she's not writing, she loves to deadlift, rewatch Game of Thrones, and drink far too much coffee.

Born and raised in America, Jenna now lives in England with her husband and her two dogs.

www.jennawolfhart.com
jenna@jennawolfhart.com
tiktok.com/@jennawolfhart

TREASON

From the past comes magic, from the present, danger, gradually colliding.

Trust no-one

That was the advice of King Adeone's father, Altarius, as he lay dying.

Trust no-one: not your friends, not your family – love them but don't trust them. Danger and betrayal can come from anywhere, from anyone.

With bereavement stalking the corridors of power and treason brewing in the taverns of Oedran, what was once safe is threatened, and the ancient magic might not be dormant.

If trusting his friends is dangerous, trusting Sergeant Wynfeld might be madness but Adeone needs all the help he can get. Friends betraying him are the least of his worries when his brother has plans…

Copyright

Copyright © J.A.Cauldwell, 2024. All rights reserved.

No part of this publication may be reproduced, distributed, or transmitted in any form or by any means, including photocopying, recording, or other electronic or mechanical methods, without the prior written permission of the publisher, except as permitted by U.K. copyright law. For permission requests, please email contact@pennodpress.com

The story, all names, characters, and incidents portrayed in this production are fictitious. No identification with actual persons (living or deceased), places, buildings, and products is intended or should be inferred.

Book Cover and Illustrations by J.A.Cauldwell

Pennod Press First edition, 2024

3 5 7 9 10 8 6 4 2

ISBN (Paperback): 978-1-917145-04-6
ISBN (ebook): 978-1-917145-03-9

Trigger Warning

This book is set in a pre-Victorian-inspired world with elements of fantasy. It includes references to difficult themes such as loss, hardship, and moral dilemmas. Some events explore the consequences of harm, ꞏꞏtal oppression, and personal struggles, including grief and guilt.

ꞏꞏok is written in British English. The lack of Z might keep you ꞏꞏt we like U. If you prefer a different flavour of English, I ꞏꞏnd your next read soon.